Café Noir

A Collection of Mysteries from the Coffee House Writers Group

Featuring:

Maria A. Arana
Tim Cassidy-Curtis
Robert Joyce
Michael Kramer
Mary Steinbroner Lugo
Scott McClelland
Wolfgang Shane
Elena E. Smith
Rick Stepp-Bolling

Edited by
Wolfgang Shane

Assistant Editor
Tram Le

Cover Art by Christine Marie Bryant

Table of Contents

I believe writing is a way of self learning. Writing promotes growth, it's self therapy, a reflection, a productive outlet and a direct conversation between ego and soul. It's magic that we are capable of. I love that writing is a chance to be heard, an opportunity to be validated and an escape.

Writing is also one of the most amazing tangible things that we leave behind after our time here is done. Our written words become a legacy of our stories, our thoughts, our emotions and our imaginations of who we were.

I want to encourage all of that.

Christine Marie Bryant
Coffee House Writers Group President

First, thanks to all you readers who purchased this book. Your support is amazing and humbling. Thanks to all the authors who participated. We couldn't have done it without you. Thanks to Steve Harshberger for his technical expertise. Thanks to Christine Marie Bryant for having the vision to make the Coffee House Writers Group a reality.

Special thanks to my assistant editor Tram Le for all her tireless efforts. You are incredible!

Wolfgang Shane
Editor

Introduction

There's nothing like a good mystery. Who did it? Why did they do it? What really happened? Is it justice?

This anthology is a collection of short stories whose central premise is a mystery. The authors, some new and some seasoned, are all members of the Coffee House Writers Group (CHWG), a non-profit community that exists to assist writers. CHWG holds regular meetings, workshops, write-ins, and other events to support its mission of offering a safe and nurturing environment for writers to flourish.

The Coffee House Writers Group is a 501(c)(3) non-profit organization. If you are interested in joining or learning more about CHWG, find us on Facebook or our website at www.chwritersgroup.org.

Wolfgang Shane
Editor

Tram Le
Assistant Editor

A Game of Hearts

by Mary Steinbroner Lugo

"God, oh God! The pain! It hurts! Make it stop!" Fingers clenching in agony, scrambling for the call button as eyes fly open, searching for aid.

A face comes into focus.

"Help! Help me! Please!" a voice sounds, barely above a whisper.

No help is offered. Death comes, only death.

***

The text came in late.

Sharon, there's been another one. Can you meet me early AM at FarWest Community – Lina

Lina was my contact with the police department. When something odd came up, they contacted me. I am a forensic pathologist, and I try to help when the PD is puzzled.

Holliman—Sharon Holliman—doctor.

Didn't sound as good as "James Bond," but I liked it.

I sighed as I looked at David sitting in my lap. At six, he was trying his best to talk me into buying him a pet while doing his math homework.

"Mama, if all the apples are gone, why should I bother? If we had a pet, I'd name it Max, and I would feed him and walk him and take really good care of him!" The words ran together as fast as he could talk.

I nuzzled David's freshly bathed neck and dialed my mother.

"Mom? Could you keep David longer for me? I need to go into the field. Thank you so much!" It was going to be another late day tomorrow.

I tucked David into bed as he continued his con.

"And a pet would keep me company when you're gone. 'Specially at night, Mama."

"I know, baby. I know."

***

Early the next morning, I hurried into the morgue, patting the DNA scanner as I went.

"Where's the body, Lina?"

A small woman with intricately braided hair motioned me to a graying cadaver. Lina's detective's badge was fastened on her belt, under a thin protective coat that covered her street clothes. I added a similar protective coat over my clothes and looked where she gestured. The corpse had the traditional "Y" cut. Lina stepped back, letting me view the damage.

"The pacemaker disintegrated just like the other two," I noted. "It damaged the heart, resulting in sudden death."

Why? Thoughts quickly tumbled through my mind as I absentmindedly rubbed the small scar on my left breast. My own pacemaker. It helped a heart that was the product of bad genetics.

I looked at Lina, shook my head. "Go ahead and have the coroner close her up. Nothing left to look at." I sighed, tossing the protective coat into the recycling bin for the next poor schmuck who had to use it.

***

Working with the PD and the hospital gave me some leeway and enough clout to access the medical files and ask questions. I scanned the files and learned all of the recipients of the pacemaker were elderly, over 60, and had common heart problems exacerbated by smoking, stress, and other outside effects. Two men, then the last one, a woman, Barbara Richardson. Their standard background checks didn't find anything to tie them together. The manufacturer of the pacemaker *was* the same so that seemed the best place to start.

Several phone calls later, I had an appointment with Dianne Christenson, MD and PhD. She had patented the technology for this state-of-the-art pacemaker, cunningly called the "Versaas." The FDA had found no obvious problems with this machine once R&D had worked out the bugs. I couldn't help but wonder if there were some "lemons" in the mix.

A tall, willowy blonde slowly rose from behind the antique mahogany desk, as stately as a queen greeting her subjects. She took my card, glanced at it, and tossed it on the desk.

"The police are looking into *my* pacemakers?"

She clearly looked down at anyone in her realm as minions, and I was no exception. "My pacemakers are superior to anything on the market, and they passed the FDA's most stringent tests." She paused, for effect. "In fact, they passed with such high marks the FDA couldn't believe it and tested them again! So *Ms.* Holliman, if there are *any* problems, it's the surgeon's fat hands that are causing them."

The good MD and PhD escorted me to the door of her "throne room," clearly finished with our audience.

I could hear her mutter, "Stupid, uneducated bitch," just as a second voice called from down the adjoining hallway.

"Dr. Holliman? Dr. Holliman!"

I looked in search of the voice and suddenly found myself wrapped in a warm hug. Margo! A student of mine from when I taught at the university.

Needless to say, I was petty enough to hope the *good* MD

slash PhD had swallowed her tongue, and nice enough *not* to turn around to watch her do it.

***

The late afternoon sun had just started its descent when I wandered back into the hospital. FarWest was the premier hospital for cardiac care. People traveled from around the world to have their hearts repaired. Most organs could be grown in a lab, which had left the worries of waiting, risk of donorship, and the lifelong dependency on rejection medication behind. As I brushed the DNA scanner to gain admittance into the hospital proper, my eyes searched the scheduling board for Dr. Michael Williams. He had performed the surgeries on two of the people and was such a good friend he wouldn't mind the questions.

According to the board, Mike had just finished surgery. I found my way over to where I knew he would head, glimpsing the nurses scanning the QR code at the end of each bed in the ward. The handheld scanners updated information for the medical personnel that would come on the next shift. Everything was carefully monitored down to the last vial of medicine and syringe used. Simple body scans were done to prevent anyone from entering the room with "extra" medication. The hospital had also included matching patients to their DNA for an extra layer of protection. I caught up with Mike outside the break room. His thin form, the slow invasion of balding, and bright eyes behind wire frames only emphasized the compassion and focus he was known for.

"Holliman!" His voice carried in a loud blast down the area. "What brings you into the land of the living?"

Mike paused and then ran his hand through hair that wasn't there.

"The pacemakers."

He sighed deeply. His face drooped in dismay.

"Sharon, I've looked over all of the cases. You know John Caros was the surgeon on one?"

I did.

"I even brainstormed with Richard, and we both agreed that there was no reason for the pacemakers to fail." Dr. Richard Kennan was Chief of Surgery and Mike's life partner. "You're welcome to have access to all of the information about the recipients."

Mike scrubbed his tired face with his hands and looked at me sorrowfully. He took it hard when his patients didn't flourish. I couldn't help but feel sorry for this sweet man, and touched his hand.

"We'll figure it out," I whispered. Then, turning around, I left the hospital, playing all the ideas and scenarios in my mind. Specifically, why the pacemakers would disintegrate at all.

***

A week later, and life repeated itself with a text.
Sharon, Another one. This makes 4. - Lina
I sighed as I sat up in bed. Soft fingers caressed my neck.
"What's wrong, babe?"

I often reveled at how those long fingers would have been more appropriate playing a piano or bowing a violin. John Caros and I met over a heart. Mine. His signature red stethoscope swinging into view was the first thing I saw as I came out of the anesthesia. After that, we stayed in touch. Shortly, a diamond found its way to my finger, and we got together when time allowed, which it rarely did.

"Is it the case? Another patient?"

I nodded. "I have no idea why this is happening, and it's making me nuts!" I couldn't help but laugh at my irritable child routine. David would have been impressed. "Too many people are dying because the pacemakers are exploding. Poof!" I gestured with my hands, then ran them though my mess of hair.

John looked at me and wondered, "It would be excruciating! It's odd. Patients didn't call for help? Machines didn't immediately detect the anomaly?" He paused thoughtfully. "Nothing and no one intervened?"

I shook my head. "Why so curious?"

I could feel his laugh land with a puff at the base of my spine, interrupting his sensuous travels. He came around and faced me; his fingers traced the line of my ribs. His kisses urged my mind to follow the lead my body had already taken.

"Just think, I could be Watson to your Sherlock Holmes," he said, his kisses becoming more heated. "Dr. Watson. It suits me!"

"John, please, I'm already focusing too much time on it during the day, and now it's filling my nights. Not a good thing."

I relished the movement of John's fingers on my tight neck muscles. John's lips replaced his fingers and moved from the back of my neck, to my jaw line, and down to my shoulder. From then on, we forgot about anything regarding hearts—except our own.

***

David woke us up early, bouncing excitedly on his tiptoes. His new kitten, Max, squirmed in his arm. David loved John's visits. He watched with curiosity as John readied to leave for his office at the hospital, red stethoscope already in place. John rubbed the top of David's head and gave me a quick chaste kiss. We both had made a promise of doing this again sometime, maybe dinner, when our schedules were free.

"How is the search for your birth parents going?" I laid my hand on his arm, wanting a few more seconds with him.

"I've stopped for now," he replied. "Dad, and then Mom, you know, my adopted parents, dying so close together last summer took the wind out of my sails. I guess Mom just didn't want to live after Dad died." He touched his forehead to mine. A sweet kiss followed. "It seems obscene, somehow, to look for a new set of parents after losing those that were so wonderful to me."

John paused, quickly bent over, and whispered in David's ear. A red licorice whip appeared in John's hand, and he palmed it off to David. As I watched him leave, I looked down into a pair of brown eyes sparkling impishly.

"Not until after dinner, young man." I rubbed Max's chin, causing her to purr, and grinned.

***

At the hospital, shouting and cursing roared out of the operating room.

"God damn it! Nikki, bag this and call Holliman!"

I tapped the DNA reader with my palm as I rushed into Mike's office. He met me holding a bag flat on his hand to keep the pieces of what was clearly a pacemaker in place.

"I was doing an emergency appendectomy on one of my patients," he said without preface as he rose from his chair and paced. "She was going sour, and we had to work quickly. All of a sudden, as I'm closing, things start smoking and sparking. I found this baby and pulled the battery. It seems to have survived. Pissed me off! It was a good unit going in. What the hell happened to it?"

I gingerly took the bag from Mike and held it level to keep all the components in place. It was covered with the normal blood and membrane of a human body. I couldn't see anything suspicious and knew I needed something stronger than my eyes to get a better look at it.

In my home office, I was armed with the schematics for this particular pacemaker and had Research and Development on speed dial. I had done a little cleaning of the unit but didn't want to disturb wires or the interior workings. Cotton swab in hand, I gently wiped more of the blood off and tried hard not to be bothered by the fumes of rubbing alcohol coming from the swab.

The unit was under the microscope and bit by bit I matched and cross-matched the microscopic parts until all of them were accounted for. On the face of the unit, I could see there was a deep scar. A scrape. I assumed it was from Mike's hurry to stop the pacemaker from exploding. I rubbed this area with a swab. At first, I thought it was a bit of tissue, but on closer look, it was a very tiny component that seemed to be lodged inside the face of the pacemaker.

Carefully, I dislodged the minute piece. I looked at the schematic but couldn't find a corresponding part. I speed-dialed R&D. The head of the department went through each and every part with me again. There was no part that matched the description and the placement of this tiny piece. A puzzle, another puzzle.

I tried to call John and got his voicemail, so I left a message.

"John! I've got to postpone our dinner for tonight. I need to look into something. I think I've finally caught a break." I caught myself laughing. "And yes, I'll consider you *my* Dr. Watson." Foolishly, I wanted to dial his voicemail again, just to listen to his voice. I didn't.

The piece was too small for me to make out much other than its shiny metal surface with my own microscope. I put the word out, and it was Lina who called and came through with a stronger one. I met her in the lab at the PD.

"Whadda you have there, Sharon?"

I put it under the powerful lens, one that could pick up the smallest details. We both looked at the tiny gleam underneath the lens. It seemed to be a computer chip. Wires crossed and recrossed the surface.

"What is it?" Lina asked, her dark eyes wondering at what she saw.

"I don't know. Pacemakers disintegrating and now this extra part?"

"Sharon, can you keep digging? You have more expertise in this area than my crew does, and when I go to them, I want to give them something they will understand."

***

I dug into the research of programming a chip. Little had been done. There *was* a familiar name but it had been mostly speculation in only one article, as "more research needs to be done." It didn't give me much. So I went back again to the medical information on each victim. I ran through medications, visitors, and medical personnel. Finally, I looked at the DNA on each victim, comparing it to the DNA of the personnel that came in and out of each person's room. It was a long shot, but then I saw a close match. It went against medical protocol that a doctor or nurse would work on a family member. That kind of stress made for mistakes. But here it was. Two people with DNA close enough to make them, what? Father and son? Mother and daughter? Who was it? I went back a third time to be sure. But this person had no reason for being in this patient's room. Another doctor had done the surgery, so...

Why?

Lina's office was a quiet haven for my troubled thoughts. She agreed that this doctor had no reason to be in this patient's room, but she needed more.

"I can get you what you need. Let me try."

***

My knees were weak and my hands sweaty as I walked into John's office, unsure of my welcome. He rose from his place behind the desk, his red stethoscope swinging. His arms wrapped me with such warmth. I felt so secure. I knew I had to be wrong.

"Anne told me you were coming in. I'm so pleased to see you!" he said gently. He tugged me closer, and I could hear his heart beating beneath his lab coat. Letting go, he strolled back to his desk doing a playful Moon Walk that he seemed to love performing. Sitting down, he gestured to the chair across from him. I was anxious, I fumbled with the file I brought in and knocked the receiver off the cradle of the old-fashioned telephone he preferred to have on his desk. I quickly tried to set it to rights as his twinkling eyes watched me.

I sighed and jumped in with both feet. "Barbara Richardson was your mother? Your natural mother?"

"So you discovered that." His head was down, as if deep in thought. He looked up and said, "I thought I had wiped that entry off the records." He fidgeted with his stethoscope. "Quite a find, don't you think? Discovering the whore that birthed you right under your nose. I couldn't resist!"

"But John!"

"Ahhhhh! The temptation! I actually was there two times. I wanted to see the bitch's face when I told her who I was..."

"The pacemaker...the chip?" I began putting the pieces together, very afraid of this man I loved.

"Yup! Invented that. It can be inserted in the body and stir up all kinds of trouble. How to get rid of your enemies in one simple stab," he continued, gesturing to include the whole room. "The military uses would be astounding! I initially tried it on the brain stem, but the brain is too complex to be able to do it accurately."

A cold chill passed through me as he paused, steepling his fingers together. The article he'd written had only touched vaguely on this. He had gone way beyond what he chose to document.

"That's when I hit on the idea of the pacemakers. So many people have them, and they give off a slight magnetic field. That's why *you* can't go through a scanner in the airport. You carry documents to prove you have one, and they let you through."

I knew then. His adoptive parents had both died from brain-related problems. No one thought to look closer.

"The chip is attracted to the magnetic field and attaches itself to the pacemaker. All I had to do was set off its programming with the hand scanner and whoosh! Whatever I'd programmed into that little chip happened! Like magic."

John rose from his desk, a syringe appearing in his hand as surely as the licorice whip. Pieces of his stethoscope littered the desk. He held it up by the plunger and let the sunlight play on the liquid inside. A single gold chip, smaller than a grain of sand, could be seen glimmering in the light. He walked purposefully towards me. I jerked away, tumbling the chair I had been sitting in. I found myself edging around the opposite end of his desk.

"I've gotten so far as to not need the scanners any more. Mommy Dearest was just the icing on the cake. And *so fun*! Bitch left me out in the streets to starve," he snickered. "Imagine her surprise when the Angel of Death was her darling son and you, darling, were so hot on my tail. Well, fuck her!"

"No, maybe not," he whispered to himself, "that would be incest."

John lunged at me, syringe in hand, just as Lina came through the door with several police. The needle hit my bicep.

"You got too close," he whispered in my ear as he grabbed me and pulled me near.

Crying out, I jerked away, praying he hadn't had enough time to push the plunger.

"Are you hurt?" voices asked.

My heart pounded. Gingerly I pulled the syringe from my arm. My breath hissed at the pain. I held it up to the sunlight imitating John's earlier move. There was nothing shining in the clear solution it held. I panicked! David! My parents! Was I going to die? This *couldn't* happen. Desperately, I flicked the neck of the needle where it met the syringe. A very tiny fleck of gold dislodged itself, floating gracefully.

John mumbled and ranted. I turned, headed for the door, and looked at Lina. I asked softly, "Did you get enough?"

"Yeah, I did. We could hear everything through the speaker button you hit when you bumped the phone."

I capped the syringe and carefully placed it in her hand. I moved in a haze out of the office. Tears made finding the door a little hard.

"He had it hidden in the tube of his stethoscope, each time. That way the scanners wouldn't pick up the extra syringes with the chips," I said by way of explanation, more to myself than to Lina. "I need to go."

I'm not sure why something that was just a muscle and a pump could hurt so much. I couldn't think. Heading through the door, all I wanted to do was go home to a little boy and a black kitten.

The Stones of Ascalia

by Rick Stepp-Bolling

"Are you sure these are the Stones of Ascalia?" I put on sterile gloves to examine the centuries old carvings. Any hint of moisture from my hands or the surrounding lab could damage the irreplaceable relics.

"Just the one stone," Heroc said. "The other is a facsimile of the one in Galka. We were able to replicate it with nano-tech."

I studied the replica under the macrometer. The etched stone looked remarkably like the original from Eythia. However, it was wider than the one here. The thickness of the stone was an oddity more than a concern. "And you're sure no one saw the replication process?"

Heroc stood silent, his weight shifted slightly onto one foot.

"What?" I demanded more than asked.

"Galkans found the transmitter as our man was exiting the site."

I nodded. What else could I do? He knew the risks. We all did. "Notify Monsignor he can comfort the surviving relatives, if indeed there are any." The war had taken its share of Eythians and Galkans alike, but if I had my way, that would soon end.

Heroc gave the sign of Diyos, touching his head, his heart and his stomach, and left. I motioned for Kaleb to join me. He shuffled to the macrometer and peered long and hard at the runes. "What do you make of it?" I asked as my curiosity piqued.

"Certainly it bears the hand of the same engraver. Notice the unique flair with the ending of the final word."

The flair was a curvature in the final letter that spiraled upwards. "Exactly as in the first stone." I stripped the glove from my left hand so I could adjust the setting on the overhead hologram. "Are we in agreement, then?"

The thin man squinted once more at the replica. "Yes, I believe we are."

My hands began to tremble. "Do you realize what this means?"

Kaleb stood and wiped his brow with his handkerchief. "Confirmation of the one and only true prophet," he said.

"Perhaps," I said, "but more importantly, an end to our one hundred year war with Galka."

Kaleb stared at me refusing to join in my elation. "I don't see how reuniting the stones will end our religious differences," he said. "Galka will claim the stones are a fraud. Or worse, they'll say we proved Gaya is the one and only rightful prophet."

"Does it matter if it proves Gaya or Diyos is the true prophet? The stones were blasted apart centuries ago by an unknown explosion. Galkans claimed their heritage from Gaya. We claimed ours from Diyos. We have been at war ever since. All because no one has ever recovered both stones to find the true answer."

Kaleb shrugged. "You've let your science get in the way of your beliefs. Come to whatever conclusions you want, it won't change anything."

I did not want to believe him. I wanted to think that when given rational evidence, people would make rational decisions. I wanted to think that. The scientist in me wanted that to be true. But was the schism between Galka and Eythia so deep that no reasonable evidence could mend it? "Kaleb, you're a scientist."

He nodded his agreement.

"And you're a Diyost."

He gave the sign of Diyos in response.

"What if the stones reveal Gaya is the true prophet? What if

our science proves that to be the case? How would you, as a
scientist and as a Diyost, cope with such an outcome?"

I could see the painful indecision tear at him before he
landed on safer ground.

"I am Diyost first. Nothing can change that."

My heart sank. If I couldn't convince my fellow scientist,
how could I convince a nation ruled by the church? Be that as it
may, I was resolved in this. "Bring in the translator."

Kaleb hesitated, but after a moment, he left to find the
converter. *He's a good man*, I told myself, *even if misguided*. A few
minutes later, Kaleb returned with the portable unit. "Long ago,
the language of the stones was lost," I explained. "Once the tablets
were broken, the language became sacrosanct, and rulers of both
nations forbade translations. The election of Monsignor Adam has
finally challenged that thinking."

"Thank Diyos," Kaleb whispered.

"Thank Adam," I said.

A loud buzz announced the arrival of someone at the slider.
I went to the vis screen. A man dressed in silver robes stood
outside. Beside him were two Eythian guards, both armed and
both with identical lightning bolts on their sleeves. I passed my
hand over the entry beam and the door slid open. "Monsignor
Jacob," I said as he entered. "What an unexpected pleasure."

"Adam sent me to observe the proceedings." He walked to
the stone replica and pointed at the tablet. "Is this the duplicate?"

"Yes," I explained. "We received the holo from Galka. This
stone was replicated from the original image."

"You should know I have been against this whole idea."

It was not a statement but a threat. "How can knowledge be
without value?" Monsignor Jacob, I knew, was a fundamentalist of
the strictest order of Diyos. He was a man with little vision and a
large ego.

"Knowledge without faith is a dangerous combination," he
warned.

"Faith based on conjecture can be equally dangerous," I
said. I looked over my shoulder at the guards. They stood at

attention without emotion. They were true believers who acted at the whim of the church, and I would not find a sympathetic ear with them.

"Let me be the judge of that," Monsignor Jacob said. "Get on with it."

I nodded to Kaleb. He rolled the portable translator into position beside the two tablets. After adjusting the lens, he looked at me.

"Gentlemen, you may not agree with what we find today, but rest assured, this is an important moment in the history of mankind." Although I overplayed the significance of the event, I hoped the drama might keep them from leaping to the wrong conclusions. "We have had this technology for some time now," I continued, "but the church has been reluctant to use it." I gave Monsignor Jacob a brief glance. "Since we have not had access to the second stone, our translation would only give us half of the intended meaning. Now we have both Stones of Ascalia, the conversion of these ancient runes brings with it the hope of a new future for both our nations." I doubted anyone in the room but Kaleb agreed with what I said, but I wanted it on audio record.

"Kaleb," I said, motioning to the screen, "project the conversion onto the overhead screen."

"No!" Monsignor Jacob shouted. "You will print the translation. I will see the results privately."

"I'm afraid that was not what Monsignor Adam and I agreed upon," I said. "If you want, the guards can leave the room, but Kaleb and I will stay." With this, I was adamant. I would not budge.

Monsignor Jacob studied me to see if I would waver on this point. Then he motioned the two guards outside. He turned and glared at me. "Continue," he said between clenched teeth.

Kaleb pushed the button. The lens took in the information from the two tablets. Inside the translator, the computer processed and searched for matches between modern Eythian and the runes on the stones. As with all decoders, a certain margin of error could be expected, but not enough, I hoped, to interfere with the final interpretation. A few moments later, the screen showed an image of the results. My mouth dropped open.

"What is this?" Monsignor Jacob demanded. "It doesn't make sense."

I walked toward the screen to get a better view of the translation. It offered nothing more than what I had read the first time.

"It must be backwards," Monsignor Jacob said. "Try reversing the image."

"No." I stopped Kaleb with my hand. "This is the correct alignment. See, this is where the stone was broken. The wording begins to the left and ends on the other tablet. It is in the correct order."

Monsignor Jacob edged closer to the screen. "Here it says, 'We wish to serve mankind,' but on the other stone it says, 'adding the blood of mashtou will enhance the effects.'" He turned to me. "It makes no sense. There is no continuity in the sentences from the first tablet to those of the second. And why would there even be a reference to a small, insignificant rodent?"

I hated to admit it, but Monsignor was correct. It didn't make sense. The translation was incomplete. I stared at the wording again. Incomplete. Yes, it was fragmented. Then it came to me. "It doesn't make sense because it's incomplete. There's a missing tablet, a third stone."

The Monsignor stared at me as though I were mad. "A third tablet? That's ridiculous! There are only two tablets, just as there are only two nations and two prophets, one true savior, and the other a minor servant of the cause. Diyos or Gaya. Two, not three."

"Then explain it. Why doesn't the meaning from the first tablet carry over to the second? It's as though someone had cut out the middle section. A third stone. Think about it, Monsignor Jacob, these stones go back to antiquity, but who said there were only two when they were separated? The simplest answer is that there were three, not two stones. We are missing the third stone."

Kaleb took a small disk from the translator and pocketed it in his jacket.

"Guards!" Monsignor Jacob cried. Immediately, the two

soldiers entered with their weapons drawn. "Take this man to the holding cell in Deit-Roi prison."

The guards grabbed my arms and shoved me toward the door. "What crime have I committed?" I asked before the guards gagged me.

"I'll think of one," Monsignor said. "I'll think of one."

***

I had never been in a prison before. I had only imagined what it would be like. Of course, I imagined the worst: dank cells with rats crawling over a stone bed, iron bars and the smell of urine permeating everything. For once, I imagined correctly. Prisoners of Deit-Roi were forgotten, expected to live their lives in a squalid hole and die of neglect. That meant I had an eternity of time to think about the third stone. Where could it be? Why wasn't it with the other two? And, of course, the greatest question—why were the stones split in the first place? Yes, I had time to ponder these questions and the mystery surrounding the Stones of Ascalia, but I had no answers. I heard the sound of boots on the cement walkway outside my cell.

A guard emerged from the shadows carrying a wooden stool. His unkempt uniform and scraggly beard told me his duty was not highly desired nor closely supervised. "You have a visitor," he said plunking down the stool. Then he simply walked away. In his place, Kaleb appeared. I had never been so happy to see someone in all my life.

Kaleb sat on the stool. "I'm sorry I couldn't come sooner," he said. "No one is allowed to speak with you. Apparently, you have become a very dangerous man."

It made no sense. How was I a danger to anyone? "But you're here," I said.

"The guards are not above being bribed."

"What have I been charged with?" I asked, but I knew it didn't really matter. Monsignor Jacob would be creative in this.

"Treason."

"Ah, yes. When Monsignor can't think of anything else, treason is always available."

Kaleb touched his coat pocket and leaned forward. "I made a copy of the translation," he whispered. "We can use it at your trial. As evidence."

I laughed at the notion. A trial? No, it would never happen. "Get rid of the copy," I said. "If they find you with it, it might mean your life."

Kaleb's hand dropped to his side. "I believe you," he said quietly. "A third stone is the most obvious answer."

I wanted to embrace him then. His science surfaced even though it must have been difficult for him to get past his beliefs. "Thank you." We sat in silence for a while. I tried to think of something to relieve the despair of the moment. "Do you still have the picture of your son at his first birthday?"

"How could I not?" He reached into his pocket and found his wallet. He rummaged through a sleeve of photographs until he came to the one I referred to. "Here it is," he said taking it from his wallet. He showed me the photograph of a wide-eyed young boy sitting in front of a small cake with me smiling behind him. He grinned, remembering the happy occasion.

"What's on the other side?" I asked, pointing to the photograph.

He turned the picture over to discover the heat of the wallet had glued two pictures together. He carefully peeled the other photo from the back of the party picture. "I must have sat on it," he said in explanation.

Something clicked in the back of my mind. Intense heat fusing together two like objects. Two like objects. "That's it, Kaleb. That's the answer."

"Yes," he said looking at the pictures. "I'll need to be more careful next time."

"Kaleb, the stones! When they were separated by the blast, only two stones were divided. The third, the missing stone, was fused to the one in Galka. That would explain the thickness of the one stone."

Kaleb thought about the possibility of two fused stones. "Yes, yes, it might have happened if the explosion were hot enough. And if the composition of the stone contained mineral elements." His face lit up in a broad smile. "It is possible." Then his body sagged. "But how do we prove it? It's a Galkan holy relic, guarded night and day. It already cost the life of one of our associates. We couldn't ask that of someone else."

"What if we don't have to," I said. "The transmission, it was a holo of the entire stone.

"Electromagnetic radiation!" Kaleb's excitement grew to match my own. "Yes, and what if it took a facsimile not only of the exterior but the interior of the stone?"

"See if the nano-tech can reproduce what was on the inside of the stone."

Kaleb was about to rush off when I yelled, "No!" He turned to me. "I can't ask that of you. If you're discovered, if word should get out—"

Kaleb smiled. "Don't worry, my friend. I am well aware of the consequences." Then he vanished, leaving the stool and me to ponder what the third stone might reveal.

***

I scratched another mark on the wall. I felt like the prisoner in all the movies I had seen about prison life in my youth, but I knew this was one way to keep my sanity as well as a record of my time here. The sound of boots on the cement alerted me to the guard's approach. It wasn't dinnertime yet, so I could not expect another bowl of thin broth and stale bread.

"Get up, prisoner and go to the far wall. Put your hands on the wall." I wondered at the guard's change in routine. Something different was about to happen. I moved to the wall and placed my hands on cold stone.

"Thank you, guard. You may leave the door open. I'll take responsibility." With my back to the man, I still recognized the voice. How could I forget it?

"You may turn around now," Monsignor Jacob said. "Please, sit." He motioned to the only seat in my cell, the stone bed. "I've just had an interesting talk with Monsignor Adam. Apparently, your colleague has given him new information about the Stones of Ascalia."

"The third stone," I said.

"Yes, he found evidence of a third stone fused to the Galkan tablet."

I leaned forward in excitement. "Was he able to transcribe the writing?"

Monsignor handed me a copy of the translation. "Put the three tablets together and this is what results."

I quickly read the document, my eyes poring over the words but not comprehending what it meant. "I don't understand?"

Monsignor stood rigid, his whole body a statue of intense focus. "Do you know your history?" he asked.

"Science and history go hand in hand," I said.

"Then you know that at the time these tablets were inscribed, the world was experiencing a great drought."

I knew the stories surrounding the event. "Yes, and Diyos called upon the waters to descend from the heavens, and mankind was saved."

"Our world was on the edge of mass starvation. Diyos saved us all, but not in the way we thought."

I looked at the document in my hand with greater understanding. The pieces were beginning to come together. "It's a recipe," I said. I could not believe what I was saying, but the truth was in front of me. "Diyos and Gaya were cooks, not saviors."

Monsignor waved my comment aside. "Be that as it may, you will understand why no one will ever see or hear about this third stone. What you hold is the last remaining evidence."

My hand felt the corners of the document as though I held a sacred scroll. "The war?"

"It will continue. It has become a lucrative financial venture for the church."

I nodded sadly. "Diyos and Gaya will remain disputed prophets."

"As they always will," Monsignor said. "When the people made them saints, they carved the Stones of Ascalia to commemorate their culinary greatness."

"And when the church discovered what the people did, they tried to destroy the tablets. But they survived!"

Monsignor took the document from my hands and crumpled it. "It doesn't matter, really," he said. "Things will go on as they always have." He walked toward the cell door.

"Why did you come to tell me this?" I asked.

"Although no one else will know the truth, I thought you should." He closed the door and it locked with a heavy clunk.

The Old Barrett House

by Wolfgang Shane

Weeds!

The damn weeds were everywhere!

Kristine wiped the sweat from her forehead with her gloved hand and looked around at the infestation of weeds in her front lawn.

She smiled. At least they were her weeds.

She bought the house two weeks ago in a part of California that was undergoing gentrification. While that was problematic, she was glad to get this place before prices really shot up. Her old Craftsman-style house, built at the turn of the last century, was the textbook definition of "fixer-upper." It had drafts, leaks, faded paint, plaster walls, stuck doors, and even more stuck windows. It also had a front porch, real wood floors everywhere, intricate woodwork, an honest-to-goodness basement, and the kind of charm you couldn't find in the cookie-cutter houses built today.

It also had weeds, lots of them, and gophers.

She shifted over to her left and worked on another patch of weeds. She didn't mind the work. Her dad, a major in the Marine Corps, raised her to be self-reliant and self-sufficient after her mom died. He believed in tough love, with equal emphasis on TOUGH and LOVE. He expected her to do well and pushed her hard, but she knew that she was everything to him.

She looked at the porch with its white fence and imagined sitting next to her dad and her husband, John Cho, watching their gorgeous kids playing in the front yard.

"*Hola.*"

A voice interrupted her daydream. She turned to see an old Latina woman carrying a bag of groceries. Kristine smiled at her.

"Hi," said Kristine.

"This house, you just buy?" asked the woman.

"Yes, I did," said Kristine. She got up, brushed the dirt off her faded jeans, and walked over to the woman.

"My name is Kristine Le," she said, taking off a glove and holding out her hand. The woman took it and smiled.

"*Hola*, I am Carmen. I live four houses down."

"Good to meet you. How long have you lived in this neighborhood?"

"*Ay Dios mio*, more than fifty years. We move in just after we get married."

"Wow, that's a long time."

"You like house?" asked Carmen.

"I love it! It's filled with wonderful little touches like woodcarvings on the crown molding. It has a mirror with an engraved wooden frame built into the hallway wall. The rooms have shelves and the day room has a bench. It's got a nice backyard and a huge basement that's almost as big as the house."

Carmen frowned. "You go basement?" she asked.

"Sure. I plan on turning it into a Woman Cave."

"You live alone?"

Kristine was a bit surprised by her bluntness.

"Yes."

"Then you are careful in basement, *si*?"

Kristine frowned. "OK, but why?"

Carmen made the sign of the cross. "The house, is haunted."

"Haunted?"

"Yes, haunted. I know the family who live here before you. They hear strange noises at night. Doors and windows open and close. They tell me is haunted. I say go to Father Lopez to bless house, but they no listen. After only six months, they sell the house."

Kristine knew the previous owners had the house for only a short time, but she figured they were just trying to flip it to make money. Carmen put down her groceries and held Kristine by both shoulders.

"You go to Father Lopez. He bless house."

"Um. I'm sorry, I'm not Catholic," said Kristine, "and I don't really believe in ghosts or evil spirits."

"You don't know," said Carmen. "I know. A Mr. Gilbert Barrett own the house before we moved to here. He catch his wife with another man. They say he took them to basement and he kill them, and now they haunt the house."

Carmen made a sign of the cross again.

Kristine nodded. "OK, I'll keep my eyes out for anything unusual. If I need Father Lopez, I'll let you know."

Carmen nodded. "I pray for you."

Kristine smiled. "Thank you."

Carmen took her groceries and went home.

Kristine looked at her house. Evil spirits? The only evil she saw was the weeds. She went back to work fighting the ravages of nature.

Three nights later, a crashing sound woke her. She slept in the upstairs master bedroom, and the noise came from downstairs somewhere. She grabbed the MP9 in her nightstand and pushed in the half-loaded magazine. Her dad taught her how to fight and shoot a gun when she was growing up. "I'm not always going to be around to kick your boyfriends' asses," he said, "so I expect you to do it when I'm not there."

She got out of the bed, holding the gun in front of her. The wood floor creaked as she walked to the door and listened. There was something. A squeak? A groan? Hard to tell. She opened the door and walked down the stairs, clearing the rooms one at a time like her dad taught her. She got to the kitchen and saw a broken glass on the kitchen floor. She flipped on the lights and looked around.

The kitchen was small by any standards. It had a patched hole in the plaster ceiling where the original wood stove had vented out its fumes. The counter was small and uneven. She remembered leaving the glass on it, but not close enough to where it could fall off. She looked at the open window. It was too small for anyone to get through so she had left it open to get fresh air in the house. Maybe a cat? A thirsty cat could have climbed in and knocked over the glass. That was probably it. She closed the window and went back to sleep.

The next weekend, Kristine finished the front yard. She also met a few more neighbors. They were mostly Latino, and many lived here for decades. On the whole, they were friendly. She went out Saturday night with friends and came home late after a night of karaoke and drinking. She kicked off her shoes and passed out on the couch.

BOOM. BOOM. BOOM.

The pounding woke her up. She looked around.

BOOM. BOOM. BOOM.

That noise was coming from somewhere. It sounded like something in the pipes. She turned on the lights and listened. Nothing.

She got up and the floor creaked. It was cold against her bare feet. She checked the front door, and it was locked. She grabbed her keys and made a fist with the keys sticking out between her fingers. One good punch would send an attacker reeling. She checked the house and once again found nothing.

She spent the next week decorating the house. She found an oak roll-top desk for the small sitting room next to the entrance and made that her office. It had built-in cubby holes that were perfect for storing stuff. She put a plush rug in the hallway in front of the full-sized mirror with engraved edges. She bought a stained oak table at a yard sale and went to work re-finishing it. She enjoyed working with her hands.

Two nights later, a creak woke her. She lay still in bed and heard another creak. She turned the light on. Another creak. She grabbed her gun. Nothing. She cleared the house again and found nothing. What could it be?

The next morning, she went around the house to look for

possibilities. There must be some way a cat or raccoon was getting in the house. She noticed a small open window in the tiny upstairs bathroom. That was a possibility. The window was stuck open so she decided to block it with plywood. She checked the basement in the back of the house. The entrance was an old-fashioned door built into the ground that opened to stairs leading down to the basement.

The haunted basement?

She took a close look at the basement. It was seven feet high and windowless. A switch at the base of the stairs turned on a single bulb hanging from the center of the room. One corner had a water heater, another an old workbench, a third had some rungs that must have held shelves at some point, and the last corner had a dark stain on the concrete floor. She felt it. It wasn't wet and nothing came off in her hand. It was old and could be anything. Varnish...paint...blood. She looked around the room again. The floor was concrete and the ceiling was rafters and pipes.

The pipes?

She looked at them. She knew high water pressure could cause pipes to clang. Maybe that was it. That and a cat would explain everything. She went to Lowe's and bought some plywood and a water pressure gauge. She blocked the window and checked the water pressure. It was normal.

Three nights later, she heard moaning. This time she was scared. The other noises were normal noises that could be caused by wind or animals, but no wind or animal could make this noise. It was real moaning. She turned on her lights and gripped her gun. She cleared the house again and found nothing.

The basement?

She went outside and opened the door. It was dark. She crept down the stairs to the light switch, holding the gun...

"AAAAAAAAAHHH," something screamed from inside the basement.

She gripped her gun and took the last few steps to reach the light switch. She flipped it on and saw...nothing. The basement was just as she left it a few days ago. It was empty. What caused the scream? She held the gun in front of her and looked around. She felt the discolored stain on the concrete floor. It felt wet. Could it just be morning dew?

She went outside and closed the big door.

The next morning, she made coffee with a shot of scotch to calm her nerves. She was sure she heard the scream. It came from somewhere in the basement, but nothing was there. Was it her imagination? Could it have been the natural noise of a house settling? She didn't think so. The plywood covering the upstairs window was still in place. It was no cat. She decided to lock up everything for the next few nights.

A week later, she woke up when she heard a thud. She once again grabbed her gun and went down to clear the house. She found the window next to the front door open. That wasn't possible. The window latched from the inside. No one could open it unless they were in the house with her. Her heart raced. She felt sweat on her upper lip. She turned on all the lights in the house and locked the open window. That night, she didn't sleep at all. The next morning, she called her father.

"Major Le," said the voice on the other end.

"Hi, Daddy, it's me,"

"Kristeenie weenie, how are you doing, sweetie?"

She did something she hadn't done in a long time. She burst into tears. Her dream house was turning into a nightmare. She didn't believe in haunted houses, but she couldn't explain any of this. Through her sobs, she told her dad what happened.

"Alright, sweetie," said Major Le. "Just calm down."

"Daddy, I don't know what's happening."

"I don't either, sweetie. You have to figure it out."

"What if the house is haunted?"

"It's not haunted."

"How do you know? Maybe it is."

"It isn't."

"How can you be sure?"

"Because haunted houses aren't real. I don't believe in them."

"Just cause you don't believe in them doesn't mean they're not real."

Major Le scoffed. "Honey, let me tell you what I believe in. I believe in the United States Marine Corps. I believe in God and country. I believe in discipline and hard work. I believe that with the right attitude you can overcome any obstacle. I believe the most beautiful sight I've ever seen in my life was your face when you were born. I believe that you are the best of your mom and me. I believe that you have her brains and looks and my determination and will. I believe that there is a logical explanation for everything. And I damn sure don't believe in haunted houses."

Kristine stopped crying.

"If you want me to come by for a few days, I'll put in for a leave."

Kristine smiled at the phone. He always knew what to say. He was all about tough love, showing both at the same time.

"No, Daddy," she said. "Let me try to figure it out."

Four days later, she woke up when a door slammed. Once again, she grabbed her MP9 and checked the house, once again finding nothing. She went to the kitchen door that was now open and inspected it. Nothing was unusual about the door, and she could find no reason why it was open. She looked around for some kind of logical explanation. She walked around the house, the wood floor creaking as she crossed it. She looked down on the floor and found the answer.

She needed to talk to her dad.

A week later, an alarm sounded on her cell phone. She woke up and looked at the screen. The outline of two ghostly figures moved across it. She grabbed her gun and cell phone and ran down the stairs. She had practiced her path to make sure that the floor would not creak as she made her way through the house. She passed the roll-top desk in front of the mirror and reached the back door to look out the window. The backyard was empty. She unlocked it and went to the basement entrance. She looked at the screen on her phone and could see the two ghostly figures glowing in infrared in one corner of the basement. She got the tire iron she hid in the bushes next to the door and put it across the door handle, locking the ghostly figures in the basement.

Now she would have some fun. She swiped across her phone and brought up an app that controlled household appliances. She hit a button, and a siren went off in the basement.

Two boys screamed at the top of their lungs. She heard them run from the corner of the basement, up the stairs to the door. They hit the door and pounded on it, but the tire iron locked them in. She hit another button, and lights flashed in the basement. Screams of terror filled the night air. She pushed another screen button, and the lights went out, the siren sound stopped, and the sound of a barking dog bellowed out. Screams for help erupted from the basement.

Kristine smiled and called the police.

Moments later, the police had the two boys in handcuffs. The two brats looked to be about fifteen years old and were shaking. The shaking got worse when their parents showed up.

"I intend to press charges," Kristine told the police. "They broke into my house several times and spied on me. They also stole a Macbook Pro and jewelry."

An officer who looked like Channing Tatum nodded his head. She lied about the Macbook Pro and jewelry, but the spying part seemed likely. She figured the least she deserved was a new computer.

One of the mothers stepped up. "We'll pay for the missing computer and stuff."

"What about spying on me! Those little perverts belong in jail!"

The mother shrunk back and did not answer.

"How did you find out they were in the house?" asked the officer.

"I've been noticing strange things happening since I moved in. I thought it was a cat or raccoon. Then it got worse. They nearly scared me to death. The last time they broke in, I figured out how they did it. I bought a thick rug and I noticed footprints that weren't mine facing away from the mirror. The only logical explanation was that somehow somebody came through the mirror. It has a decorative fringe, and I realized it must open somehow.

"The mirror was above one of the corners in the basement. That corner had rungs in the wall. I thought it was for shelving, but when I looked at the corner, I noticed an access door hidden in the rafters. The rungs were there to climb up to the door. Once I found the opening, I discovered a crawl space to get to the pipes between the walls and between the stories. It has two openings, one to the mirror and another one to the master bedroom. I also found a peephole in my bedroom."

The boys looked down to the ground.

The officer turned to the boys. "How did you know about the crawlspace?"

The boys didn't answer.

"Tell him!" commanded one of the fathers.

One of the boys trembled so much he could hardly speak. "We didn't mean nothing. We were hanging out in the basement before the other people bought the house. It was empty for a few months. We found the opening in the basement and we were just messing around."

An officer took the boys away in a police car, followed by their parents. The Channing Tatum look-alike finished his report in Kristine's kitchen. She noticed his nametag said Officer Barrett.

"Can I ask you a question?" he said.

"Sure."

"How did you get that infrared equipment and alarm stuff."

Kristine smiled. "My dad's in the Marines. He has access to all kinds of cool stuff."

"It sure scared the snot out of them boys."

Kristine laughed. "That was the point."

"Would you like to go out for a drink this weekend?" he asked, his eyes making quick contact with hers and then darting away.

Kristine smiled. "Sure, but I don't even know your first name, Officer Barrett."

"It's Gil."

Murder in the Barrel Room

by Michael Kramer

*O thou invisible spirit of wine, if thou hast no name to
beknown by, let us call thee devil!*
— *William Shakespeare,* Othello, Moor of Venice
Act 2, scene 3, ll. 300 -302

"Smell the fruit," Mart said, his nose just clearing the rim.
Brenda tilted her glass.

In the tasting room, Mart and Brenda had just sipped the
Mourvedre when the police interrupted.

"Excuse me, ladies and gentlemen. I need your attention.
I'm Lieutenant Patrick Conant of the Temecula police, and we have
a situation."

That rapidly ended the buzz of conversation and the clink
of glasses on the granite-topped bar. Everyone turned towards the
doorway.

"We've cordoned off the building. Officers are at the exits.
We'll need to detain and question all of you briefly. If you'll just be
patient, several of our detectives have set up in rooms nearby. Our
officers will call you out to interview you one by one so that you
can answer just a few questions. As I said, we are sorry for the
inconvenience, but the situation demands such extreme measures
and attention."

Of course, the rumors started immediately.

The blonde twenty-something woman next to Brenda, a member of a bachelorette party, breathed, "Do you think someone was murdered?"

Her companions stood wide-eyed at the thought.

The balding retiree next to Mart perked up and said to the woman near him, "I heard there's a serial killer."

Quickly, the quiet that followed Lieutenant Conant's announcement gave way to a buzz, its details indecipherable in the tasting room. Three sides of the room held that same rose granite countertop, corners open for the servers to access the back of the bar and the wine racks on the wall. Well over thirty guests had lined those counters just moments earlier, their largest concern whether to taste red or white.

After glancing at the clock on the wall, Mart looked to his wife. "I guess we're not going to make our dinner reservations at 6:00."

She shook her head, light accenting her red hair and the strawberry curl that sometimes fell over her forehead. "We'll explain what happened. Think they'll hold the reservation?"

In mere minutes, rumors Mart heard ranged from the earlier murder to speculation about domestic and foreign terrorism.

A rugged man, someone who worked out, spoke with authority. "*Sharia* law disapproves of alcoholic beverages. This whole place," he gestured, "shoot, this whole valley, must be offensive. You know, they're building a mosque down towards the freeway."

"If this place and its wine are so offensive," a younger man picked up the thread, "why would they want a mosque here?"

As the police took the first few people from the tasting room, a thirty-something woman near Mart stared at her smart phone.

"What's up, Tanya?" asked one of her friends, a little heavy-set but notable for cascades of wavy dark hair. "What's on your phone?"

Mart and Brenda listened as Tanya showed a picture. "It is murder. Look at this."

People craned to see her screen. After a moment, Brenda opened the same page on her phone. Looking around, Mart saw others had the same idea.

"Wow," Brenda said.

Mart found himself looking at a post on the winery's wall: two pictures posted twenty-two minutes earlier. The first showed an obviously drowned body on the floor of one of the stainless steel fermentation tanks still wet but emptied of wine. The second showed the hand-written label of that tank, "*Chardonnay*" crossed out, "*Malmsey*" crudely written over the top. Clearly murder was the crime the Temecula police were investigating.

"Apparently, the winery's Facebook page allows postings from employees as well as customers. These two are from Ashley. She works in the barrel room. But the man, I wonder who he was," Brenda said. She flipped through a few of the other postings. "There he is, I think."

She handed her phone to Mart. He saw a picture, two men together, both with winery polos, arms around each other's shoulders. The caption read, "Chief Vintner, Giovanni Batisto, with Assistant Vintner, Sunrise Peak Vineyards, Tom Smallwood."

She asked, "The face on the right—Tom Smallwood. That's the dead man, isn't it?"

Mart flipped to the earlier picture, then back. He nodded. He passed back her phone.

"But *Malmsey*—I don't recognize that varietal."

"It's a European red. I think from Madeira? Europe identifies wine by the region. The varietal here would be Tempranillo or some other Spanish red grape."

She smiled, "I'm always impressed by the stuff you know, but—"

"Shakespeare. *Richard III*. George, Duke of Clarence, is murdered by being drowned in a butt of Malmsey. His brother Richard arranges it. Historically, George tried to overthrow his brother King Edward. In the play, Richard is eliminating rivals."

"That's interesting."

Mart and Brenda looked over the bar. The server had been listening.

"So," Brenda looked at the server's name tag, "Hayden, have you ever met Mr. Smallwood?"

"Well, yeah. We meet most everyone connected with making the wine. I've been here seven, no, almost eight years. For us servers, they have mandatory meetings weekly. The vintner-bigwigs go over the different varietals."

"So, Smallwood?"

"Yeah. Nice enough guy. This is really a shock. Just this past Monday, Smallwood talked to us. He was launching a new line of sparkling wines, all from Sunrise. The sparkling Chardonnay you tasted earlier was his first release."

Brenda scrolled to the picture of the tank with the body. She handed Hayden her phone. "So was this one of his tanks?"

Hayden took his fingers and enlarged the top of the picture. "Yeah, it was. See the area towards the top? No lines for valves. That means the CO_2 stays in the tank. A simple and effective way to carbonate our sparkling wines is to keep the CO_2 in the tank. That's the Charmat method. Real champagne is produced, *méthode Champagnoise,* bottle by bottle." Hayden shook his head. "Drowned in his own vat."

"Couldn't he have fallen in?" Mart asked.

"Not really." Hayden handed the phone back to Brenda. "That other picture? The date? That's today. That tank was filled this morning with the squeezings from yesterday. The only way in is that hatch on the side. Someone had to force him in there."

"No wonder they've sealed the place off." Brenda looked around wide-eyed. "The murderer's likely still here. Maybe an employee, someone trying to blend in with the customers?"

Others had listened in on Brenda's conversation with Hayden. Soon the whole room buzzed, and Mart watched as people seemed eager to move away from strangers.

The police took another group out of the tasting room.

Brenda continued looking at the pictures. "Hey, Hayden.

Another question. Look at the body's lips, in the picture. Something's there making them pucker like that." She pointed at the screen.

Again, Hayden took the phone, enlarged the picture. "Weird. A muselet."

"*Muselet?*" Mart asked.

"The little wire cage that holds the cork on sparkling wine. I guess that's an effective gag. Keep him from shouting."

Brenda shook her head. "I'd think that would be really hard to get on the mouth of someone still alive."

"You're right, ma'am. You're right."

"That means he was dead before he was put in the tank. He didn't drown."

Mart, Hayden, and a number of others around them understood and nodded.

Brenda seemed entranced by the winery's Facebook page. Mart listened as snippets of conversation swirled around them.

One woman in a short tight dress spoke emphatically. "I bet he was fooling around with one of the family's wives. You know this place is family owned. Still, I just don't buy all those family pics and how happy everyone looks," she told her friend, equally poured into her dress. Her friend nodded.

A twenty-something guy with jeans and a Burning Man t-shirt, said, "But what a way to go. Dude. Drowning in wine. I mean —"

His girlfriend, perhaps a little bored with him, said, "But it wasn't fermented. That means no alcohol. Like, he drowned in grape juice."

"Sweet," someone else said, waiting for the joke to register.

Mart shook his head and turned to Brenda. "What are you looking for?" he asked.

"A lot of pictures, different employee events, show Tom Smallwood. He shows up a lot more than the head vintner. Giovanni Batisto's hardly anywhere."

"Maybe, as an Italian—" Mart began.

Hayden, still standing near them at the bar, interrupted.

"Nah. Giovanni's about as Eye-talian as me. *John Batisto*'s on his driver's license. Moved down here from Napa."

"Oh?" Brenda looked up.

"Yeah. Batisto knocked around a few of the wineries up there after graduating from Davis. English minor."

"Well," Brenda continued, "Smallwood shows up a lot. He seems to schmooze a lot with the winery owners."

Hayden nodded.

Brenda looked up to the ceiling. She pointed. "See the writing on the rafters? More Shakespeare."

The beam above them read "A man cannot make him laugh – but that's no marvel; he drinks no wine. — Shakespeare."

"I think that's from one of the Henry plays," Mart speculated.

"That's all Giovanni's doing. Said his major kept him looking for quotations. He said everyone knew Shakespeare," Hayden responded.

"Mart, we need to talk to that Lieutenant Conant." Brenda looked at her husband.

He cocked his head, an eyebrow raised.

"I know who murdered Smallwood."

Mart explained to Hayden. "She reads a lot of mystery novels. She's probably right. Usually solves the mystery at least a hundred pages before the end."

Hayden smiled and nodded.

Mart took Brenda by the hand and pointed their way towards the door.

Brenda pulled back. "A minute," she said. She looked to Hayden. "What did Giovanni think of the new line?"

"Wasn't impressed. Called it 'soda pop.' Said it was a disgrace to the winemaker's art."

She smiled. She looked to her husband. "Let's go."

Less than ten minutes after Brenda told an officer that she needed to talk to Lieutenant Conant, the stocky detective arrived at the door.

"Yes, ma'am? You need to speak with me? Something about

a murderer?"

Brenda suddenly seemed bashful. Mart picked up. "My wife says she knows who killed your victim."

"I don't recall any announcement about a murder," the lieutenant responded.

"Are you kidding?" Brenda blurted. "It's all over Facebook."

The lieutenant escorted them out into a small office near the gift shop.

Seated behind the desk with Mart and Brenda on the other side, Lieutenant Conant smiled. "Tell me your theory."

Brenda looked to Mart. He shrugged.

She began, "Okay. So Tom Smallwood, the assistant vintner was your victim. You found him in a tank just filled this morning with juice from Chardonnay grapes. But the label on the tank had been crossed out and re-labeled 'Malmsey.'"

"All that's on Facebook?" The lieutenant shook his head.

"But see, it wasn't Malmsey. They don't make any wine called *Malmsey* here. Mart, my husband, he teaches English. Mart says George, Duke of Clarence, was murdered in a barrel of Malmsey."

The lieutenant appeared confused.

"*Richard III*. Shakespeare." Mart tried to smile.

The lieutenant glanced back to Brenda.

"See, Hayden—he's a server in the tasting room? Been here for years. Anyway, Hayden says Giovanni," she looked at Mart. "But he's not Giovanni, is he? He's John Batisto who graduated from U.C. Davis with an English minor. He's responsible for the Shakespeare quotes the winery uses." She picked up an empty bottle from a credenza in the office. "See? 'Come, come, good wine is a good familiar creature—Shakespeare,'" she read. "Anyway, John apparently didn't think much of Smallwood's new line of sparkling wines. Maybe he was feeling like his job was threatened. Maybe they fought..."

The lieutenant smiled. "Mr. Batisto is a person of interest. One of the workers in the fermenting room identified the writing on the card, your *Malmsey*, as that of the Head Vintner."

Brenda acted surprised at the lieutenant's revelation. She nodded and swallowed. "And the muselet."

"The muselet?" again the lieutenant appeared confused.

"That's the little wire cage which normally holds the cork on a bottle of sparkling wine? The Facebook picture showed one on the victim's mouth," Mart explained.

"We hadn't made that public. Facebook?" he looked from Mart to Brenda.

She nodded. "Yes."

"I've got to get my people on social media."

"Well, the muselet wasn't to keep him quiet or anything. It just fixed his lips in a kiss, the way my grade school kids do their lips when they call someone a kiss-up."

The lieutenant pursed his lips and nodded. "Makes sense. We hadn't thought of that."

"And George, Duke of Clarence, drowned in a vat of wine."

"The play. *Malmsey*," Mart explained.

"Begins to make more sense," Lieutenant Conant smiled.

"Batisto felt threatened, so he killed Smallwood, wired his lips out of anger at Smallwood's kissing up, shoved him in the tank, and began to fill it up," Brenda spoke triumphantly.

Lieutenant Conant nodded, picking up the thread. "I wonder if anyone heard the two arguing. I think we can announce that all of you in the tasting room can go home. We've pinpointed the time of the murder to before the winery opened to the public, and we've used the monitor with the director of HR here to be sure no employees, except for the servers of course, were in there with you. As I said, the Head Vintner, Giovanni Batista, was a person of interest. You know, if it hadn't been for the word *Malmsey* and Smallwood's shoelace stuck in the door, the body might not have been found for months."

"A horrific way to ruin a batch of wine," Mart added.

"Gross." Brenda wrinkled her mouth in distaste.

The Little Lamb Ruby

by Tim Cassidy-Curtis

The door was a perfectly secure vault door. The viewing room was a five-foot-wide perfect square, perfect dimensions for a perfect viewing room. The walls were one foot thick and perfectly sound-, light-, and everything-else-proofed. On the walls were vistas of perfectly done holographic scenery. There was a perfectly smooth bare floor. In the center was a perfect pedestal. On this was a perfect cube. Inscribed at the lower edge in perfectly neat hundred-point script was "THE LITTLE LAMB RUBY."

The cube's perfectly clear material was intended to perfectly show off its contents.

I looked at the empty box. "Oh," I said, "This is just perfect."

"Welcome to the Little Lamb Ruby Display," intoned an automatic announcement. It played a pre-programmed recording in six different languages. "This gem is the largest of its kind and has a distinctive inclusion that has an image of a sheep. Under normal light, absorption qualities of the ruby render the inclusion a black color. However, after storage at cryogenic temperature, the inclusion takes on the image of a white lamb when illuminated by a laser. No other gem in the world has this feature."

The recording droned on. "The Little Lamb Ruby is the

property of the Kingdom of Caspian Persia and is considered a priceless national treasure."

And now it was gone.

Half of Caspian Persia's economy came from tourism, this ruby being a prime destination. A contralto voice seemed to come into my left ear. That was Lance, an artificial intelligence in a super computer under Cheyenne Mountain. *The growing prosperity is the only thing keeping reactionary elements in the society at bay.* I was looking at more than the economic collapse of a country; I was looking at its disintegration.

I reflected upon my assignment. I got the call shortly after midnight, which would have been early morning here. They were, quietly, a U.S. regional strategic ally. They merited US support, quietly—me. I was briefed and on my way in four hours. In another four hours, I was in country, since I have access to the fastest transportation in the world. Two hours later, I was at the facility looking at an empty transparent box because I had to take the slowest transportation in the world. It was late afternoon, local time. While I contemplated the scene, I felt that I was not alone.

"Commander Snell!" I heard a deep mellifluous tone. Lance flashed the essentials of a dignified six-foot-two gentleman with sharp scholarly features. I quickly learned all I needed to know about this gentleman.

I calmly turned around and saw a short stout woman. *Very funny, Lance.*

"The Director will see you now," she said. She had a deep voice, which could be mistaken for masculine but had a sensuous silky quality that was unmistakably feminine—once you knew who was speaking.

I had Lance record every detail of the room and followed my escort. Bhai-Auki Vonda-Liana Val-Ala-Barristan was the First Assistant and had a doctorate in physics.

She led me to a modest office with some chairs and a desk. Behind it sat the man Lance had previously described. The only difference was the profound worry lines on his face.

The current crisis seemed to have aged him by ten years. He was dressed in a nice but unpretentious suit. He was typing on his desktop when we got to the door and did not acknowledge us as we entered and stood directly in front of him.

"Thank you, Vonda," he said, without looking up, and continued to type. She continued to stand there; the look on her face seemed to expect something more. He hit the enter key and barely glanced at her. She gave me a "See how he is?" look and plopped herself in a chair. I sat in another chair without further ado. His nameplate read AARON ZENO, PHD, DIRECTOR.

He finally looked up with a satisfied huff. "Forgive me, Commander," he preemptively stated. "I was expecting the United States to send several experts, not just one person."

I said nothing. Instead, I took a small sticky sheet and wrote "LANCE," followed by several numbers. Then I handed it to the Director. He looked at it, gasped, and tossed it into the shredder.

"That," I told them, "is why you want me here. You are familiar with the Logic and Notarization Computer Emplacement?" They nodded. Lance rarely referred to himself by his full nomenclature. "I have a chip that allows instant access." The look on the assistant's face was cryptically intriguing.

His bank account was a nice touch, I thought to Lance. *But did you really have to include his niece's bra size?*

Zeno's lips pursed, and he nodded. "Well," he said, "this should be easy for you to solve."

"Indeed," I replied, "I already solved it."

***

The Little Lamb Ruby display room was filled to its capacity with the three of us in it. Only a few people were allowed in the room at the same time for viewing and security reasons. Doctors Val-Ala-Barristan and Zeno were on either side of the six-inch-wide pedestal. I stood by the wall, directly under one of the holographic outdoor scenes.

There were several inconspicuous controls on these scene displays. The principles worked on lasers, which was how I had figured out the caper. Lance had taken a detailed picture of the room and brought to my notice microscopic lines in the transparent box in which the Ruby was exhibited. They were invisible to the human eye; thus, the transparency of the glass cage was unmarred in terms of public display. I had Lance analyze the pattern, and something remarkable appeared.

I adjusted the display's laser settings. Suddenly, the Little Lamb Ruby appeared.

"This is a hologram," I said. "It is an extremely accurate representation of the actual object. To the casual observer it is impossible to tell it from the real thing." I started to gather steam. "The culprit would need knowledge of how these things worked and high-level access to accomplish the switch. It would have happened yesterday morning." Heads nodded. I kept going. "There is only one person who could have done this." I looked directly at the Director and the First Assistant. "Only one person has the technical and scholarly capabilities. Arrest Doctor Val-Ala-Barristan. You will find the ruby somewhere on her premises."

Remember when you were young? You got these incredible insights that seemed to be so brilliant that everybody would think you're a genius? You marched right into the most public spot you could find, and boldly made your declaration? You expected adulation, praise, applause. Instead, you got something else. I heard crickets chirp.

Aaron cleared his throat. "The hologram is a design feature to help us position the ruby. The security cameras have sensors that detect objects on the pedestal. Vonda has been with me since last evening a few hours after we closed the display. It was somewhat early, we had a power outage." He looked me in the eye. "She couldn't have stolen it."

I looked at Doctor Zeno. He looked calm and cool.

Doctor Val-Ala-Barristan was another matter. She

stormed out without another word.

***

"You must leave," Doctor Zeno said without preamble. I wanted to object, but he continued. "Our economy rested on the ruby. Hostile forces inside our kingdom will soon act. You will not be safe. Also, you falsely accused a member of my staff. Perhaps you understand if I have no interest in protecting you."

Worry lines added another five years. "Make no mistake, we will not cover this up. My report will be presented to His Majesty prompt—"

Things went dark. Well, somewhat darker. It was early in the summer evening, and the remaining light softly suffused the entire facility. Director Zeno sighed, "It is another power outage. We are still a developing country, and our infrastruc—"

The lights came back on. Zeno looked at his computer and sighed again. He'd have to rewrite his report.

"Perhaps the King will understand a slight delay."

***

In the end, I reckoned that I had until close of business the next day. I spent the rest of the day, late as it was, inspecting the crime scene. The cube was still firmly attached to its pedestal and still empty. The crime scene tape had been removed hours ago. Forensic examinations were complete and reported no fingerprints except for that of the staff.

It was getting late. The outer corridor glowed with the last rays of the day. All visitors were long gone; I was alone. Per procedure, the holographic scenes were turned off. It was just me, the empty box, and the pedestal.

I felt a temperature change. I saw the erstwhile empty cube fill with what looked like water.

Artie! If a computer could cry out, it would sound like this.

It looked like slow motion. The vault door slammed shut, and the room sealed. I was a fraction of a second too late.

I looked at the box. Its top opened, and the contents started to boil. *That's not water,* Lance said, *that's liquid nitrogen.*

The small viewing room rapidly chilled.

The temperature, Lance announced, *is dropping rapidly.*

"How cold?"

Minus eighty, Fahrenheit. Lance had just pronounced my death sentence. *The ruby is stored in liquid nitrogen overnight, and the room temperature, chilled as it is, reduces the overall energy demand. The low temperature maintains the effect of the inclusion. Thermal stresses, caused by differential expansion-"*

"Lance!" I interrupted. "Freezing! Can we get a signal out?"

No, Lance answered. *There seems to be electromagnetic interference.*

"Ah," I said. "Something just right to prevent the function of a 'chip?'" My rueful smile was marred with a chilly tremble. My cold-slowed brain recalled that Dr. Zeno's doctorate was in art history. I had a possible suspect.

"Can you do anything with the temperature?"

Yes, Lance said, *there is a small adjustment—three degrees.*

I shivered, violently. It was hard to think. Despite the freeze, something tickled my brain. "Do it!"

Ice formed on the walls. "That's not water, is it?"

No, was all Lance said. Carbon dioxide had frozen out of the atmosphere. I was getting woozy and losing track of time.

In a temporary moment of lucidity, I saw a bare wall. No ice. Then it hit me. Everybody thought rocks could not evaporate into thin air. I would prove them wrong.

"Is there any way to override the programming and open the door?"

Yes, Lance said, *but it is protected by a very sophisticated encryption. I'm trying a rotating cypher.*

"A rotating what?" I asked. The chill was putting the brakes on my brain.

Imagine a shift cypher, Lance patiently explained. *You replace one letter with another by shifting the alphabet. Shift by two and "A" becomes "C." Now, imagine the shift for each letter is different number. The key is the amount you shift each letter. If the key starts with a "C" that letter gets shifted by three, so for example "L" becomes "O."*

"Huh," I chattered, "but you would have to guess the key sequence." My brain lugged. "Lance ... you're ... not ... good ... at ... guessing. I ... not ... enough ... time... here." My cognitive level plummeted, so I held an image in my mind. Only one person would have the educational level to attempt jamming a chip in my head. With a name thirty-three characters long, it made an excellent cypher key. Lance had me out in a cold New York minute.

I had Lance check the room's records. That's where I found it—a slight pressure rise, and a minor imbalance of atmospheric composition, both followed by a small temperature adjustment of just under three degrees.

***

The auctioneer stood up one more time and regarded his audience. It was the low end of the high end. The event was indistinguishable from any other respectable auction. The clientele were respected businesspersons. There was tea and coffee, but not all the snacks were food.

Their entry list was a computer printout—a piece of cake for Lance to include my name.

"Ladies and gentlemen, there is one item that has been added at the last minute. The item is a ruby, one of the largest in the world. It has a dark inclusion of intriguing shape. Specifications are on your electronic pads. Who shall start the bidding?"

There was an audible gasp from the audience, and bids

started erupting at five digits.

We began with twelve bidders in the room and six on the phone. As bidding entered six digits, four were left in the room, including me, and three on the phone. When bidding reached seven digits, there were two on the phone. I heard one other person in the room. Bidding passed eight digits, and it came down to the voice on the phone and me. I listened intently and noticed the caller was using a machine that masked voices.

That's probably the thief, I thought to Lance. *He's bidding on the item he stole in order to hike the bid.*

I've analyzed the voice mask. It is typical of the S800X. That model was known to be one of the most sophisticated. There was no way to determine the voice behind it. *There is one vulnerability.* Lance continued, *when there is a power loss it defaults to a standard mask. The reset takes a quarter of a minute.*

Well, then, I thought back, *I think it's time for a black-out.*

No sooner had I had the thought when things went dark. Well, somewhat darker. The early afternoon sun diffused onto the scene and illuminated an Auctioneer who appeared concerned but not surprised. Momentary outages were common.

"Ladies and gentlemen, please forgive this interruption. It will be only a moment."

I recited to myself. "Mary had a little lamb, its fleece was white as snow, and everywhere that Mary went, the lamb was sure to go." It took fifteen seconds, and then the lights came back on.

Now, I thought, *let's hope the call is local.*

It is, said Lance, *I have an address, right here.*

Ah, I replied, *Then you know what to do. We may be able to identify the voice, but that won't ensure a conviction. We need to catch the thief red-handed.* I chuckled. "Red-handed." Get it? *Ruby. Red.* I got the impression that Lance did not appreciate my sense of humor.

They're on the way. Lance wasted no time. *Artie, you must hear this.*

The un-masked voice sounded masculine, but with a sensuously silky quality.

I knew that voice. It wasn't a man.

Suspect apprehended, Lance reported. *Now let's make that "red-handed."*

I hate Lance's sense of humor.

I had won the bid. As a condition of the auction, I had the right to prove the goods were genuine. So long as I didn't damage the item, I could do anything, but suspected everyone would be rather cool to my idea.

I took the ruby and put it into a clear-sided box. Then I poured in liquid nitrogen; I heard gasps. It sat there at the bottom of what looked like a glass box filled with water. Any other rock may have had a problem, but I knew this one could just chill.

"As everybody knows, objects subjected to low temperatures get smaller. This is called thermal shrinkage." Heads nodded, albeit nervously. "This shrinkage will also put pressure on the dark inclusion that you can clearly see." The ruby sat there, unaffected.

"This shrinkage, and the pressures that it causes, creates an interesting effect when illuminated by a laser."

I reached for the low-power laser that had just the right frequency and aimed the laser at the heart of the ruby. Suddenly, there it was.

It was a little lamb; its fleece was white as snow. Officials were summoned. It was over.

Almost.

***

I squeezed into the Director's office with Doctor Zeno, Doctor Vonda, and a couple of law enforcement officials. Zeno looked incredulous but somewhat relieved with the return of their national treasure. Vonda appeared stubbornly ingenuous and continued to insist on her innocence. The law enforcement officials seemed patient, but clearly that was limited.

"You won't be able to prove a thing," Vonda finally said.

"The Little Lamb Ruby was actually stolen the night before." I looked at Director Zeno. "She was late, wasn't she?"

"Yes," he said.

"The ruby was replaced with a fake, crafted out of dry ice. She put it into the box and filled it with liquid nitrogen to keep it from sublimating. It looked like it was still there. Later, when she made sure she had an alibi, the liquid nitrogen boiled off and the fake ruby disappeared. An examination of the pressure and composition of the air in the room substantiates this." Heads nodded, it was all falling into place.

"At the auction, our thief was not only trying to sell the gem, but was also bidding on it in order to hike the bid. I had agents at the address. They listened for conversations. They found something very interesting."

I played the recordings from the auction.

"We will now subtract the masking from an S800X." When that happened, everybody heard two identical recordings. It was almost impossible to tell them apart. "You will find an S800X Voice Masker, with that exact setting and fingerprints of the accused."

The Inspector made a quick call. After a couple of questions, he raised his eyebrows, said, "Thank you, good bye," hung up, and cuffed a now stunned Dr. Bhai-Auki Vonda-Liana Val-Ala-Barristan.

***

So, the "chip" story? Lance mentally nudged me.

"The truth is supposed to be technologically impossible," I pointed out. "Quantum entangled particle clusters shared between a computer and a human."

Yes, Lance summarized. *Telepathy.*

Who Done It?

by Maria A. Arana

Clamp. Clamp. Clampety clamp.

The sound had reverberated in my eardrums for the past ten minutes, preventing my sleep. A few miles back, a nail had wedged itself into the tire and there seemed to be no end to the darn clanging.

The car came to a jolting stop and I bumped my head into the window. Welcome to the crime scene. Brushing my hair back in place, I watched the patrol car's lights and the uniformed officers chase the civilians out of the way.

"We are here, Chas Aussenac," my partner, Ea, said.

It sat with shoulders against the seat cushion, hands on lap, and eyes engrossed on the scene outside.

"Listen, you don't have to go around detailing my freakin' name." Undoing the seatbelt, I secured my Dickies jacket. "Chas will do."

"Very well, Detective Chas."

Exasperated, I pressed the side door button and let myself out. Apparently, the self-driving car forgot to unlock us. The DMV's going to have a field day with the report.

Only four steps toward the building, and I spotted Officer Muro, a petite woman with hair braided back. She greeted us, but kept her gloved left hand on her gun, which hung on her hips like a tutu.

"The body's over here, detective." She turned, and I followed behind, glancing at her well-polished black shoes and the perfect crease of her pants.

I pulled out my pen and pad from the inside pocket of my jacket. "Does the victim have a name?"

"Will Ramirez." She cocked her head and pointed to the deceased with her thumb, nails trimmed to the hilt.

Raising an eyebrow at the familiar name, I stopped and stared at the back of Ramirez's head. My father had busted him years ago. What was he doing out here?

"His wallet was filled with hundred dollar bills and a piece of paper with a long number," Officer Muro stated.

"A number?" I spotted the turned over hand stained with blood.

"An activation number?" Ea knelt and used its camera eye to photograph the victim's face. "The suspect is wanted for armed robbery."

"Ea, this is a victim of homicide." I scratched my head. "You know, murdered."

Standing, Ea observed the body and then turned to me. "A suspect is one that has not been caught. This man has not been arrested and tried."

The artificial intelligence furthered my exasperation, and I scratched my temple, hoping the mere act would end the nausea.

"I don't have time to go into this shit." I waved my hand in dismissal. "Take a look at the number in his wallet, and see if you can run a match on anything." I turned to the officer who licked her plump dry lips before covering them with her fingers from amusement. "Okay, how soon can the M.E. give us the stats?"

Muro tilted her head, then, turned to my partner with a slight grimace. "She's over there with the forensics team."

Ea grabbed the victim's stiff arm and raised it. "For the record, I would like to mention that this man died of a heart attack. Not from the—"

I slapped my forehead. "Just get the info on the number, Ea. Let everyone else do their thing here."

Staring blankly at me with those glass amber eyes, Ea moved away from the body. Built-in to his forearm, Ea had a computer he used to access data at high speed.

"Geez," I managed to say, shaking my head.

Someone cleared her throat behind me. I turned to spot a very attractive brunette with red highlights facing me, wearing a full-fledged black uniform. Her glasses curved at the edges and she had a slender neck I swear I could wrap one hand around.

"Detective Aussenac? I'm Doctor Tasha Do." She removed her gloves and extended her hand.

Taking it, I said, "Tell me he didn't die of a heart attack, please."

She pushed her glasses back and cleared her throat again. "It appears he did, but I have to open him up to make sure when those wounds were made."

Nodding, I pulled out the mini notepad from my back pocket.

"That could get lost," she said airily, glancing at my ancient technology.

I flipped the notepad open, and mumbled, "Not you, too."

I jotted down how the victim was found and the details she gave me. Each time I gazed up, Doctor Do relocated long strands of dyed red hair behind her ear. I placed the pen in my mouth thinking about why everyone had an issue with paper and pencil and who wanted a deadbeat like Will Ramirez dead, until I sensed Do's eyes fixated on me.

She smiled, and her glasses slid down the bridge of her nose.

Was she—*flirting*?

But that irritating whir of Ea's voice saved me from finding out.

"The activation number is for a software program."

"Great, Ea." I looked away from the medical examiner and made my way to it. "Whose?"

Ea stood tall and stopped blinking. "Unknown. It has not been installed on the purchaser's computer."

My face contorted into a frown. "What program and whose?"

"Los Angeles County."

With my mouth falling open, I held my breath. Maybe the number was to hack into the system and reinstall the program with their specifications. God, I hated updates. Worst would be if Ramirez was just a decoy for a larger scheme someone was cooking up for the force.

"What if this number's been leaked?" Officer Muro asked.

Her intervention snapped me back to the case.

"Okay. Let's say this number was left on Ramirez to divert us from the killer." I stuffed my notepad in my pocket. "And let's say this number isn't functional at all, only an activation code the killer wants us to plant in the department."

"Too many speculations, Detective Aussenac." Ea locked eyes with me. Its spotless skin shone under the light, devoid of expression. "The suspect was working for someone in the department."

"Who's speculating now?" I raised my arms. "This guy's been dead like—"

"Five hours," Doctor Do projected her airy voice.

"Right." I nodded.

At that instant, Ea pulled out his firearm and pointed the thing at us.

"Whoa, partner." I got in front of Muro, whose hand already made for her Beretta handgun.

"Since I inputted the number in my system to check for matches, I can no longer make sound judgments."

"What the—" I took a step back, almost bumping into Officer Muro.

"Who decided to give A.I.'s guns anyway?" she commented as her finger tensed on the trigger.

Nearby, the screeching of tires coupled with the clampety clamp of metal burst its way through the windows.

We all covered our faces from the impact, except Doctor Do, who ended up running as far from the vehicle as possible.

With a tic to his neck, Ea said, "I apologize in advance for my actions, Detective Aussenac."

Then, Ea pulled the trigger, and I fell against Officer Muro. My shoulder burned and throbbed. Stunned, I brought my hand to the new hole in my body. Dizzy from the impact and my partner's compromised circuits, I couldn't seem to apply enough pressure.

Ea climbed onto the car and shouted, "Who done it, Detective Aussenac? Who done it?"

Through gritted teeth and squints, I rolled off Officer Muro, who couldn't get a shot.

The car opened its door to let Ea climb in. The doors locked and bystanders ran for safety on the streets. Without delay, he sped away with the patrol cars chasing them.

Muro secured her gun and leaned to apply pressure to my wound.

Doctor Do brought over her medical case and tore open a wad of gauze. She inserted the fabric into my hole. Creasing her forehead, she asked, "What's that thing talking about?"

Hissing at the pain, I took a deep breath and wiped my chin. "'Who done it' was a phrase my father used to say." I let out a groan as she taped the gauze in place. "A phrase when he caught the criminals."

Doctor Do placed more gauze and had Officer Muro remove my jacket, then asked, "So, what's that got to do with Will Ramirez?"

The memories of my father were buried since the funeral. I had forgotten how much they hurt. He'd wanted me to become a policeman and join him in the force as soon as I was able, only to shun me in the process. Now, those words he used to say rang in my ears, and I moved away from the doctor.

She reached for me. "We need to get you to a hospital."

Ignoring her, I moved further away and dragged my feet past the debris from the window. My breathing got ragged and sweat formed on my face and armpits. Tripping on Ramirez's arm, I caught sight of a card sticking out of his sleeve that wasn't there before.

My heart somersaulted, and I wiped my chin. I looked up at Officer Muro and Doctor Do. I glanced at the bystanders outside in shock, covering their mouths or trembling as the officers directed them aside. At that point, I pulled the card out and turned it over. The blood drained from my face, and my hand shuddered.

Who done it, son?

The Answer

by Elena E. Smith

When she opened her Facebook page, she saw the notification she had hoped for. She darted the mouse to her inbox. "How did you find me?" she read.

She stared. He wrote back. She had hoped he would, not with a question, but with an explanation. Her mind raced. He read her message last night, hours after she posted it. Hours after she had gone to sleep. And even if she adjusted for the difference in time zones, well, he was still reading his mail very late at night. He was probably married. A Facebook profile with no relationship status was always suspect.

When he signed on later tonight, he would see that she had read his message, whether she responded or not. She knew he was not online right now. No green dot. He was probably married.

What should she say? Just the truth? Or draw things out for a while? Post a picture? Well, if he looked at her profile, he would have seen the pictures. He just didn't know the significance.

She kept staring at his name and let memories wash over her. She'd searched for him many times over the years, but didn't find him until the most recent attempt. She had forgotten that although everyone called him Sam, his real name was James. If she had remembered that, she would have found him years ago. A big so what. It was too late to make a difference.

When she first saw his photo, it didn't look like him at all.

He was a swarthy, portly man with glasses. But when she looked through his profile pictures, she found a shot of him at twenty-seven—slim, with long curly black hair. Her heart thumped.

What did he see on her page? A former hippie chick turned corporate with grey-streaked hair, a zaftig woman wearing the Lagen look? Phoenix versus L.A. They were both so different now, but were they?

She had to decide what she wanted to gain from this transaction. Reconciliation? That wouldn't work. He'd never leave the desert for the big city. An explanation? It would be a start. An apology?

Then the green dot appeared next to his name. Oh, crap, he was online right now! And he could see that she was online. Damn. No time to think. Her finger raced to the attachment button, and she sent him the picture of a beautiful young lady with black curly hair.

"This is your daughter," she wrote.

Then she deleted her Facebook account.

Trunk

by Elena E. Smith

She was pretty for sixty-two: tall, thin, athletic, with blonde highlights. No one looking at her would guess that she'd just won the Lotto. That was why she was driving alone from Phoenix to L.A. on I-10 in the dark.

She'd been visiting her favorite sister in a whitewashed suburb when she got the call from her husband, Bill, early in the morning. "Honey, you'll never believe it." At first, she didn't.

She wanted to fly home, to claim their prize immediately and start making plans. Get out of debt. Buy a nice car and a house. Yes, a house in a safe, upscale neighborhood away from the people who never took care of their lawns.

But she couldn't fly home. She'd driven her car here.

"How fast can you hit the road?" asked Bill. "It's too hot to go through the desert midday. You should leave fourish, and you'll be here by eleven."

He made reference to her numerous potty-stops, and they both chuckled. Other than those annoying calls of nature, she would drive straight through, she assured him. But by nine-thirty, she was too hungry, and there was a huge truck stop at a freeway junction up ahead.

She parked as close to the restaurant's front doors as she could but not close enough to a light pole. She looked around. It appeared to be safe. She didn't mean to be paranoid, but she had hoodlum neighbors for so long that every man she saw made her jumpy.

The food was good, hot, and fast.

Back at the car, her key stuck slightly in the lock. What the...? She jiggled it.

A large hand clamped down on her left arm; the right smothered her mouth. A tall hard body pressed her from behind. "Don't make a sound," the raspy voice warned.

Her captor grabbed the keys and tossed them backward. She heard her trunk pop open. As he held her close, his left hand reached away, and then came back. Duct tape covered her mouth, and a pillowcase stifled her. She felt his body twist toward the back of her car.

"Take her purse," he ordered.

A second man grabbed it, and she recognized the scent of a deodorant or aftershave. Maybe this would help the police catch him, if she got away.

She didn't fight as they stuffed her in the trunk, banging her head, her shoulder, and her shins against the edge. They tied her hands behind her back.

Inside was hot and stuffy. The driver door slammed. The engine revved. She contorted her body and wriggled her tied hands in front of her. She took off the hood.

There was only one reason she cooperated. These men had taken her purse, but her cell phone wasn't in it. It was in the front pocket of her cargo shorts, pinching against her waistband. She withdrew it and adjusted her fetal position to view the screen. No missed calls. No matter.

She had watched TV shows where a cell phone's GPS could pinpoint someone's location, and she was relying on Hollywood stories to get her out of trouble. She would call Bill, and he'd call 911. He already knew she was in San Bernardino County because she had told him where she was right before she ate dinner. Maybe she even gave him the name of the truck stop; she couldn't remember.

Her right thumb pressed the number one, auto dial for Bill.

No problem with the connection from inside her prison, thank God! On the screen, she could see it connect. Then, she heard an unexpected sound from inside her car. A cell phone was ringing.

iPhone uPhone

by Scott McClelland

Justin, what are you doing here?

You know me, Suzy, I love a party. You look surprised.

Well, it's just—it is a surprise, isn't it? A delightful surprise?

Is Samantha here?

Samantha?

Yeah, I thought she'd be here already. Have you seen her?

Uh, no, not here.

Wow, thought she'd get here before me.

Really? Well—you're here. And that's—great, right? Isn't that great?

Yes, and let me say that you're looking radiant, Suzy.

Thanks, Justin, and you look so umm—can I get you something to drink?

Do you have that Santa Rita pinot?

I do. What a great memory you have. We also have fresh juice: pineapple, mango, watermelon. And we have cucumber water.

I'll stick with the pinot.

Okay, Justin. All right. I'll be back.

***

Dale, what the fuck is he doing here?

I have no idea, Suzy. He's supposed to be locked up in a hospital.

Well, he's not. And he asked for wine.

That's ridiculous. What did he say?

He's looking for Samantha.

You're kidding?

Not kidding. He's your friend, Dale. Deal with him.

All right. Jesus, it's not like he's running around with a meat cleaver.

Get him out of here.

***

Justin. The J-man. What's up, dude?

Dale, great to see you.

You, too. Just-in-time.

Ha. You'll never let that one go, will you?

Never. Put'r there, pal. So, what's going on, man? We thought you were—uh, your phone is ringing.

Oh, just a sec, I have to take this. It's Samantha.

It's Samantha?

Yeah, just give me a minute.

Okay.

Hey, baby, thought you'd be here by now.

Why would I be there?

What? Who is this?

Who were you expecting it to be?

My wife. Who're you?

You know who I am.

Okay, funny. Can I talk to Samantha please?

Wouldn't you rather have a muffin?

Look, stop kidding around, pal. Put my wife on the phone.

I have blueberry, chocolate chip, poppy seed—

You're calling from my wife's phone. Quit fucking around, and put her on.

Fucking around?

I don't know what kind of game you think you're playing—
It's no game.
Okay, that's it. Hand my wife the phone, right now, or I'm calling the police.
Where would you send them?
What did you say?
Where would you send the police?
Okay, fine. Excuse me, um, pardon me, Terri?
Yes?
Your name's Terri, right?
Yes.
I'm Justin, you worked with my wife, Samantha. I'm Dale's friend.
I know who you are.
Okay, good. Can you call 911 for me?
911? What's wrong?
Some guy is on my wife's cell. He just called me. He's on the phone now, and he won't put my wife on and—I need you to call the police, okay?
Did you ask Dale?
I'm asking you, Terri.
I still think we should ask D—
Call them right now!
Okay, okay, I'm calling.
Thank you, Terri. Did you hear that, pal? We're calling the police.
Bad idea, Justin.
Who the fuck are you?
—Umm, yes. Hold on . . . Justin?
Is that 911?
Yes. I'm not sure what the nature of your emergency—
Thank you, Terri. Can I use your phone?
Well . . .
I have to tell them what's wrong, Terri? Come on.
Okay, take it. Just take it.
Thank you, Hello?

Yes, sir, what's the nature of your emergency?
I need the police to come here.
What's your location, sir?
5161 Hedge Grove Court.
And what's the nature of the emergency, sir?
Well, this person—this man—he's on my wife's cell phone. He's still on it. He called me, and he's being very umm—I'm just going to step outside here—he's not telling me where my wife is, and he won't say how he came to have her phone.
All right, sir. We have a regular patrol in that area. I'll send them to your location now.
Okay, thank you. Thank you very much.
Can I have your name, sir?
Justin, and my wife's name is—
Is the address your home, sir?
No, I'm at a party. A friend's house.
Have you tried your wife at home, sir?
We don't have a real phone. Just cell phones.
All right, sir. A deputy is on Hedge Grove now. Do you see a sheriff's cruiser?
Yes, I do. That was fast. Thank you so much.
Not a problem, sir. I'll stay on the line until the deputy is with you.
That's okay, he's here.
Okay, sir. You have a good evening.
Thanks again. Did you hear that, pal? The cops are here.
Justin, you shouldn't have involved the police.
We'll see about that, won't we? Hello, officer.
Is this your property, sir?
No, my friends are having a party. The reason I called 911 is this guy. He's calling from my wife's cell, and he won't tell me why he has her phone, or where she is, if he stole it or anything.
This man has your cell phone?
No, my wife's phone.
Could it be some kind of prank, sir?
I don't think so.

Do you know where your wife is, sir?

Well, no. She should be here, but – could you just talk to this guy?

May I have the phone, sir?

Yes, here.

—This is Deputy Mobray, Lake County Sheriff's Department, who am I speaking with?

Oh, thank God you're there. I'm Samantha. My husband, Justin, he's not well. He's supposed to be in the hospital but—

Where are you now, ma'am?

I'm at the hospital. They called me and said that Justin disappeared after dinner.

Would you like to speak with him now, ma'am?

Could I?

Alright, I'm handing him the phone now, Sir.

Yes.

It's your wife, sir.

Oh my God, thank you. Samantha?

Justin, Justin, Justin. I told you not to involve the police.

That's not my wife. It's still the guy!

Can I ask you why you're on this property, sir?

I'm here for a party.

In this house, sir?

Yes, my friends, they're having a party.

This house is for sale, sir. Do you see the sign here? It's been for sale for more than a year now. It's unoccupied.

I assure you, officer, my friends are inside.

Did you enter this house, sir? Turn the lights on?

It's a party. There's—they have cucumber water.

Can you show me, sir.

Of course.

Justin, no. Don't let the deputy go in the house.

So you know the owners, sir?

Yes, Dale and Suzy. Friends of mine, they're in the kitchen.

Hello . . . ? Lake County Sheriff . . . I'm entering the home.

Oh, Jesus Christ—

Looks like Suzy's gone to pieces.

GET DOWN.

And Dale's off his head.

ON YOUR KNEES. DON'T MOVE.

You sure stepped in a hat full of shit didn't you, Everett?

ON YOUR FACE. SHOW ME YOUR HANDS. SHOW ME YOUR FUCKING HANDS.

Gotta say, this is one hell of a party.

DISPATCH, I NEED BACKUP, EMS—DOUBLE HOMICIDE. DOUBLE HOMICIDE AT 5161 HEDGE GROVE COURT.

Double? Have you checked the living room, Everett?

WHAT DID YOU SAY?

I said, "Have you checked the living room, Everett?"

HOW THE FUCK DO YOU KNOW MY NAME?

Don't you recognize me, Everett? I'm Justin. My wife, Samantha, worked with your wife, Terri.

Justin—? Justin—wait—you're Justin Baladan?

The hits just keep on coming.

Your wife was—

Never found.

Then . . . who?

Yes! Who, Deputy Mobray?

Dispatch, be advised, I have Justin Baladan in custody. Repeat, I have Justin Baladan in custody.

Oh mess, my phone's ringing again. You better take a look.

What the fuck?

Don't you love caller ID?

How the fuck? That's my wife's number.

Answer it, Everett.

—Terri, what's going on?

Who's Terri?

Who are you?

The Muffin Man. Do you know the Muffin Man, Everett?

Where's my wife?

In the living room, and it looks like she spilled the pinot everywhere.

Terri? Oh, Jesus—
You won't like what you find in there, Everett.
Terri, no—
You should make an offer on this house, Justin.
Oh God, Terri! No, please no—
I mean, this place has everything.

The Disappearance of Uri Chang

by Robert Joyce

So, it all came down to this. I had been here before, but it has never been this bad. I was standing in a pool of blood. Not mine, but I know the jackass across the room with a gun in his hand knew whose it was. My gun was pointed at his head, his at mine, locked in this perpetual dance of death.

"Where's the body?" I asked.

He gave no response, but his eyelids twitched.

"Put the gun down," I said.

"You first."

We were standing about ten feet apart in the run-down apartment of Uri Chang. Chang was the perp I had come to collect, but I had found his apartment in shambles, blood everywhere, and this idiot instead. It was damn hot, and we were sweating like pigs. I needed to end this situation before I passed out.

"OK, we could both put our guns down at the same time."

"You think I'm stupid or something?"

"Here, like this."

I tilted my Browning 9mm sideways and lowered it. I could see the tension in his face recede as he began to put his gun down. As soon as he turned the barrel away from me, a cat rushed through the room. Startled, he jerked the gun up and fired at me. I rolled out of the way and squeezed off a quick shot. It struck him in the center of his chest. He dropped his gun, stumbled backward, and hit the wall. He fell to the ground.

"Wat da hell!" the kid whispered, unable to shout as the bullet took his life.

Damn! I had just wanted to wound the kid. How the hell was I going to interrogate this son of a bitch now?

I stooped down over the body, patted down his sides until I located his wallet. Inside the wallet, I looked at the photo ID. Theodore Remington III, 22, 6'0", 160 lbs., black hair, and brown eyes. I looked down at Theodore, noticing his dyed green spiked hair, multiple tattoos, and piercings.

"Well, Theodore, what the hell were you doing here, and where is Chang?"

I continued looking through the wallet; he had about $200, which I pocketed. "You don't need it anymore." He had a USC ID, a few cards, and some photos of him with a younger Asian girl with long, bleached-blonde hair. Behind the photos was a folded up piece of paper. I unfolded the paper, revealing a flier advertisement for a local nightclub, The Psycho Kitty. The ad said it would be featuring the electrifying rhythms of DJ Thrash Remington this Saturday night.

Then I removed his phone. It needed a thumbprint to unlock so I grabbed his hand and placed his thumb on it. I scrolled through his recent texts. He had texted someone named Evelyn a few hours ago. They had a conversation about him stopping by Uri's and then meeting her at the Psycho Kitty at 5 p.m. I looked at his contacts and jotted down her name, Evelyn Chang, and her number.

I decided to call the cops and report Remington's death before one of Uri's neighbors called them, and some dumb patrolman tried to arrest me for murder. So I called my longtime friend on the force, Christina Carpezi.

After a couple of rings, a woman's voice with a slight Italian accent answered, "Hello, this is Lieutenant Carpezi, Homicide Department."

"Hey, Christina. It's Matt Holt."

"Matt! How have you been?"

"Well, I've been better. I'm afraid this isn't a social call. I just shot someone."

"What? You OK?"

"Yeah, I'm fine. But he's dead."

"What happened? Where are you?"

I told her I was in Uri Chang's apartment on the eastside of Chinatown because of a bounty out on him. He failed to appear in court a few days ago. Then I told her about my encounter with Theodore. She said to stay put, and that she'd be here in fifteen minutes. It was good to have friends in law enforcement.

Twenty minutes later, Christina and her officers arrived at the apartment. They quickly secured the crime scene. Christina stood in the center of the room barking out orders to her crew. Once she determined everybody was doing their job, she came over to me.

"Dammit, Matt! You know better than to stand in a pool of blood," she said, pointing at the blood on my shoes. "And did you mess with the victim's possessions?"

I didn't say anything. She knew me too well. Seriously, what would I say? "Yes, I took $200?" Best to keep quiet.

"OK, so explain what happened?"

"Like I said before. I came to Uri's apartment to arrest him. The door was unlocked, so I entered. When I did, I saw the blood, and the place was a mess. I heard footsteps, so I took out my gun. Then, Theodore came out of the bedroom with his gun drawn. We faced off for a few moments." I told her about the shootout.

"You know being a bounty hunter only gives you the right to arrest your bounty. It doesn't give you the right to kill people. When you saw the blood, you should have called the police."

"I'm sorry, but my training got the better of me. I felt I needed to take care of the situation. Besides, it all happened in just a few moments. There really wasn't enough time to call the cops."

"Ok, we're not going to arrest you. But I want you to come down to the station sometime today or tomorrow to make your formal statement," she said, sighing. "I can't help but think you're abusing our friendship on this one."

"I'm not trying to. I really appreciate your help. Speaking of help, I need to know whose blood that is," I said, pointing at the floor. "When will your lab guys be able to tell me?"

"First, my lab guys report to me, not you. And second, where do you get the nerve to ask for more help?"

"I'm sorry, but I need to find out what happened to my bounty."

"Fine. It generally takes a day or two if we have his DNA on file. Do you happen to know what he was arrested for? That would help determine if we have his DNA."

"Yes, he was arrested for selling drugs."

"Ok, I'll check with narcotics."

"Thanks for all your help." I left the apartment.

I walked back to my car, stood next to it, and took out my phone. Time to check in with my boss, Andrew "AJ" Jackson.

"Hey AJ, it's Matt."

"Matt, how ya doin? Have ya got the bounty yet?"

"No, I've run into a bit of a snag. I went to Chang's apartment. He wasn't there, but there was blood everywhere, and the place was a mess."

"Is the blood his?"

"I don't know. The cops said it'll take a couple of days to determine that."

"I think he's dead. I'll give ya a week to find the body. Then I'm gonna file a motion with the court to try to get my bond money back. Ya know if ya don't find the body, we probably won't get any money for this. I'll be pissed if I don't get that $200 grand back."

"I know," I said. My cut of that money was $20k. I'd be pretty pissed, too. "But that body could be anywhere. I need more time than a week to find it."

"That's right. The body could be anywhere. That's why I'm only givin' ya a week. I think it's long gone, and we've lost our money."

After talking to AJ, I glanced at my watch. It was 4:30 pm. I looked up the Psycho Kitty's address on my phone and linked it to my GPS. I got into my car and drove to the club. When I arrived, I was a little confused. None of the buildings in the area were named "Psycho Kitty," but there was a restaurant called Nocci with the same address. I parked and entered the restaurant. I flagged down a waitress. "Is this the Psycho Kitty?"

"Only on the weekends, sugar," she said. "That's when the youngsters use this place as a nightclub."

I glanced around the restaurant until I noticed a young Asian woman with long, bleached-blonde hair sitting on a barstool.

I strolled across the room to get a better look at her. She had excessive makeup and skintight clothes. She looked just like the girl in Theodore's photos. She sat at the bar, sipping a blue colored cocktail. She glanced up as I approached and said, "I'm not interested."

Startled, I said, "Huh? Oh, I'm not here to hit on you."

"That's good, cuz I'm waiting for my boyfriend. He'll be here soon." She twisted the cocktail straw in her drink.

I grabbed a stool next to her and sat down.

She glared at me and made a 'humph' sound, then took a sip of her drink. "I thought I told you I'm not interested. I have a boyfriend. Besides, you're way too old for me. What are you, like, 40?"

"I'm 35, but I'm not hitting on you."

"Then why are you here?"

"Are you Evelyn Chang?"

Her eyes widened, and she shifted in her chair. "Who wants to know?"

"My name is Matt Holt."

"You a cop or something?"

I'd found it's best not to answer this question with "I'm a bounty hunter." People tend to get edgy around bounty hunters. Luckily, I also worked as a private investigator. "No, I'm a private eye." I showed her my P.I. license.

"OK, so what do you want with me?"

"I'm trying to locate a guy named Uri Chang. Do you know him and where I can find him?"

"Yeah, I know him. He's my cousin. Have you tried his

78

apartment?"

"Yes, I tried his apartment."

A group of about dozen young Asian men entered the restaurant. One in the front of the pack, possibly their leader, nodded his head at Evelyn. She nodded her head in response. Then they sat down at a cluster of tables across from us.

"Friends of yours?" I asked.

"Not really. More like friends of Uri's." She took out her phone to look at the time. Then said to herself, "Where the hell is he?"

"Is your boyfriend Theodore Remington?"

Her mouth was agape. She said, "Only his parents call him Theodore. His name is Thrash. How the hell did you know that?"

"I'm an investigator. It's my job to know. You met him at USC?"

"No, he doesn't go to school. I met him at a rave. He's a DJ."

"Do you go to school?"

"Yeah, I go to CSULA. I'm studying to be a nurse."

"Your parents paying for that?"

"No, I work part-time as a phlebotomist, and Uri helps with the rest. If you know so much about my boyfriend, do you know why he's late?"

"As a matter of fact, I do. He died in a shootout at Uri's apartment a little over an hour ago."

"What? You must be mistaken! He can't be dead! Oh Thrash! What did I do?" She put her head between her hands and sobbed.

The leader of the group of men and four of his companions broke off from the pack and walked over toward us. When he was a few feet away he said, "Evelyn, this guy bothering you?"

Teary-eyed, she looked up and said, "Yes."

"You're coming outside with us," he said, and motioned for two of his companions to grab me. They escorted me through the kitchen of the restaurant to an alley behind it.

"Evelyn is protected by the Jade Dragons," he said.

"Look, I don't want any trouble. I'm just trying to locate a guy named Uri Chang. I hear he's an associate of yours."

"Are you a cop?"

"No, I'm a P.I. Do you know where I can find Uri?"

"Enough talking." The five guys surrounded me.

It's times like these when I was glad I had a black belt in Kajukenbo, but one against five was not great odds.

***

I limped past the bodies of the fallen Dragons. I went back to my car, bruised and sore. I drove home to nurse my injuries. I put on a swimsuit, grabbed a beer on my way outside, and walked to my Jacuzzi to relax my muscles. As I soaked in the tub, I heard the gate door creak open. I turned and saw a tall leggy brunette with deep ocean blue eyes wearing a white blouse and gray skirt. She strolled into my yard as if she owned the place. It was Brooke Easton, my former FBI partner.

"You look like crap," she said to me as she approached. "What happened to your face?"

"It's a long story. For what do I owe the pleasure of your visit tonight?"

"Earlier today I was working a stakeout at a place called Nocci. It's a known hangout of the Jade Dragons. Ever heard of it?"

My face turned a bit red. "Uh, yeah, I might have."

"Besides getting into a fight, what were you doing there, Matt?"

"Working a case. Maybe you can help. I'm trying to locate an associate of the Dragons named Uri Chang. Have you seen or heard of him?"

"Yeah, I've heard of him. He used to be an informant for the FBI. He stopped a few years ago and went back to his old ways of dealing drugs for the Dragons."

"Why'd he do that?"

"Probably because of his long family history with them. His father had been one of the gang's founders, but a rival gang killed him in a massacre when Uri was 15. His mother disappeared after that."

"And the stakeout?"

"We were staking out Nocci to try to find him and turn him into an informant again."

I sipped my beer. "You off work?"

She nodded."Yeah."

"Want a beer? I can get you one."

"I'll take one, but I'll get it myself. You look pretty banged up." She walked into the house, returning a few minutes later with a Budweiser in her hand. "I can't believe you drink this crap. Don't you have anything better?"

"Didn't know I was having company or I'd have picked up a nice microbrew."

"That would've been better. How's the water?"

"It's nice, hot, and soothing."

"Mind if I join you? I've had a long day and can use a dip."

"By all means. You bring a suit with you?"

She smiled, "It's only been 8 years since we were together last and you know I don't need a swimsuit."

In the morning, she woke first and got out of bed. As she dressed herself, I noticed the tattoo of a dragon on her back. "When did you get that?"

"Oh, you're awake. I got it a few years ago. I was doing some deep undercover work with the Dragons and felt the tattoo would help with my cover. Do you like it?"

I looked at her back, covered almost entirely with a green Asian style dragon. "It's very nice. You getting dressed already?"

"Yeah, I need to get back to my stakeout. I got to go." She finished getting dressed, kissed me, and left the house.

I drove to the police department to give my statement on the shooting. While there, Christina came over to give me the lab results of the blood.

"I got some odd news for you, Matt," she said. "First, the lab guys tell me that the blood belongs to multiple people, and so far none of it is Uri's."

"Whose blood is it?"

"Wait, there's more. Remember how hot it was in that apartment?"

"Yeah, it was a good 20 degrees hotter in there than outside. Why?"

"That's because someone turned the heater on. Which is odd for a hot summer's day. But, it has to do with the blood. They tell me that that blood was old. Maybe a month or two. Person who raised the temperature did so to try to make it look fresh."

"Why?"

"The lab guys are pretty sure this blood was stolen from a blood bank. They only keep blood for about 40 days, then discard it. This blood was stolen during the discard period."

With this news, I left the department. I needed to have another chat with the phlebotomist Evelyn Chang. I bet she was the one who stole that blood. But, why? And where was Uri?

I called Evelyn's number. After two rings, she answered. "Hello?"

"Hello Evelyn. This is Matt Holt, the P.I. you met yesterday at Nocci."

"What the hell do you want? This is harassment. I'm going to call the cops if you don't leave me alone."

"Feel free to do that, and I'll let them know how you stole a bag of blood from the blood bank you work at."

She went real quiet. After a long pause, she said, "You have no proof I stole anything."

"Look, I won't tell the cops about it if you just tell me where I can find Uri."

Another long pause. "Fine, you might try his mom's place."

"His mom? I thought she disappeared after his father's murder."

"Yeah, she left Uri when he was fifteen, but on his eighteenth birthday he got a postcard from her with an address near Vegas."

"Do you have that address?"

"Yeah, hold on. OK, it's 2100 Warm Springs Road, Henderson, Nevada. Are we done now?"

"OK, I won't tell the cops about the blood."

I filled up my gas tank with Theodore's money and headed out to Vegas. I made it to the city a little after 4 pm. I drove past the glitzy strip and continued driving to the suburb of Henderson. I arrived at the house. It was a tan ranch house next to a golf course.

I exited my car and was assaulted by the blistering dry heat of Nevada. I went to the door and rang the bell. A few seconds later, an Asian man in his twenties opened the door. He said, "What?"

"Are you Uri Chang?"

His face turned pale. He tried to slam the door, but I put my foot in the way. He ran back into the house. I rushed in after him. He scrambled through the house with me in pursuit. He fled out the back door and hopped over the fence onto the golf course. I jumped the fence and sprinted after him. I was a good foot taller than him, and with my larger strides I quickly caught up to him. I tackled him onto the grass by a pond.

"Please don't kill me!"

"What? I'm not here to kill you. I'm here to arrest you and bring you back to court. Who's trying to kill you? Is that why you faked your death and ran to Vegas?"

"Don't take me back there! She'll kill me for sure!"

"Who's trying to kill you and why?"

"I witnessed a corrupt cop working with the Jade Dragons. I saw her kill one of their rivals. I'm supposed to testify against her," he said.

"Do you know her name?"

"No, but I know what she looks like. She's tall, dark hair, blue eyes, and a dragon tattoo on her back."

"Crap. OK, let's get you back to the car."

I reached down to help him up when I heard a gunshot and saw a bullet ricochet off a tree next to Uri. Instinctively, I pushed Uri into the water and pulled out my gun as another shot grazed my right upper arm. I dove behind the tree. I peered out to see Brooke aiming her gun at me from about ten yards away. I tried to steady my right arm to aim at her stomach and fired the gun. My injured arm shook too much, and so my shot missed its target and punctured the left side of her chest near her heart. She stumbled backward and fell to the ground dropping her weapon.

I ran to Brooke. "What the hell? Why'd you do this?"

"I'm sorry, I was trying to shoot Uri, not you." Coughing up blood, she opened up a locket on her necklace. Inside was a picture of a boy about seven. "They have him."

"Who's that? Who has him?"

"He's—," she coughed again, "our son. The dragons have him." She gasped her last breath.

"Brooke!" I cradled her lifeless body in my arms.

After the ambulance and police arrived, I took Uri back to the car. I called AJ and let him know I'd be returning Uri tomorrow. As we drove back to L.A., my mind raced with the knowledge that I had a son and wondered what Uri knew about him.

Meet the Authors

Maria A. Arana

Maria A. Arana is a teacher, writer, and poet. She has published a personal narrative in the February/March 2013 *Animal Wellness Magazine* and a science fiction short story in the 2016 *Stone Bird Anthology*. Her poetry has been published in many online and print journals. You can find her at https://rainingvoices.blogspot.com and https://twitter.com/m_a_Arana

Tim Cassidy-Curtis

Tim Cassidy-Curtis is a science fiction writer, aerospace engineer, retired Lieutenant Colonel (US Air Force), and active Lieutenant Colonel (California State Military Reserves), historian, and is now a mystery writer. He has a life membership with the Air Force Association, Military Officers Association of America, American Institute of Aeronautics and Astronautics, and the Greater Los Angeles Writers Society.

Robert Joyce

Robert Joyce is an aspiring writer, and this is his first published story. He is an avid reader of mystery and science fiction novels. Robert earned a Master's degree in Anthropology and lives in Fullerton, CA with his wife Roslyn. They have a border collie named Jazzie, a cat named Kizzie, and four chickens.

Michael Kramer

Michael Kramer taught high school writing and literature for forty years, teaching at three schools, including a boarding school. He delights in his marriage with Rebecca. They saw their four children all move through Lutheran education and into professional careers. An advisor for Orange Lutheran's award-winning literary magazine, *King Author*, Kramer has published poems, essays, and short stories. His 2011 book *Hopeless Cases,* a collection of short stories in verse, constitutes a novel set in a boy's boarding school.

Mary Steinbroner Lugo

Mary Steinbroner Lugo has been writing since she was seven years old, exploring everything from poetry and essays, to short stories and novels. She draws on her wealth of life experience to give color to her tales. Mary attributes her continued passion for the written word, and sanity, to the antics of her five children, nine grandchildren, and three great grandchildren. She currently lives in Southern California with her private IT person (her son) and a little black cat.

Scott McClelland

Scott McClelland is a Pushcart Prize nominated author who is r comfortable in any home that has no pickles.

Wolfgang Shane

Wolfgang's interest in writing began in grade school. During religion class in Catholic school he decided to upgrade the "Jonah and the Whale" story with a talking whale. He got to the second page before Sister Killian found it and confiscated it. That was also Wolfgang's first encounter with censorship.

Rick Stepp-Bolling

Rick Stepp-Bolling is a retired professor of writing from Mt San Antonio College. Currently, he is a golfer and a full time writer. He has two books published: SMOKE AND MIRRORS (a book of poetry) and AUTOCIDE (a collection of short stories). He has finished a fantasy trilogy, PATCH MAN, the first book of which is published by Crimson Cloak Publishers. Rick lives with his wife, Francie, and their family of animals.

Elena E. Smith

Elena E. Smith is a writer and blogger. You can find her humor posts at http://grouchyshopper.com/. She is also publisher of the website Blog Indexer, http://bi-blogindexer.com/, a site that lists over 5,000 blogs in 70 subject categories. Smith blogs about blogging, at http://biblogindexer.com/about/blogs.

Made in the USA
San Bernardino, CA
25 August 2018